Imperium Press was founded in 2018 to supply students and laymen with works in the history of rightist thought. If these works are available at all in modern editions, they are rarely ever available in editions that place them where they belong: outside the liberal weltanschauung. Imperium Press' mission is to provide right thinkers with authoritative editions of the works that make up their own canon. These editions include introductions and commentary which place these canonical works squarely within the context of tradition, reaction, and counter-Enlightenment thought—the only context in which they can be properly understood.

STEELSTORM

THOMAS777

PERTH
IMPERIUM PRESS
2021

Published by Imperium Press

www.imperiumpress.org

FIRST EDITION

A catalogue record for this
book is available from the
National Library of Australia

ISBN 978-1-922602-13-8 Paperback
ISBN 978-1-922602-14-5 EPUB
ISBN 978-1-922602-15-2 Kindle

For Reagan and the Zionists, the USSR represents the epitome of evil, but for us it is a great power neighboring us with its own security requirements and a doctrine that corresponds to them.

Otto Remer

To sum it all up, I must say that I regret nothing.

I was one of the many horses pulling the wagon and couldn't escape left or right because of the will of the driver. We shall meet again. I have believed in God. I obeyed the laws of war and was loyal to my flag.

SS-Obersturmbannführer Adolf Eichmann

Part of [Von] Leers' political attitude is apparently due to his conversion to Islam, which was accompanied by a change in his name to Dr. Omar Amin von Leers. He is becoming more and more a religious zealot, even to the extent of advocating an expansion of Islam in Europe in order to bring about stronger unity through a common religion. This expansion he believes can come not only from contact with the Arabs in the Near East and Africa but with Islamic elements in the USSR. The results he envisions as the formation of a political bloc against which neither East nor West could prevail."

CIA report on the partisan activities of Johann Von Leers, October 24, 1957

PROLOGUE

LOCATION: Baikonur, Kazakhstan, USSR
YEAR: 1983 AD
DATE: December 24—warday

Tamerlan Maltsev unceremoniously tore through a cream-colored envelope that he had retrieved from a wall safe only moments prior. An innocuous thing—odd, given its contents. The envelope bore not even a security clearance designation, but only an ink-stamped, heraldic hammer and sickle atop a globe. He contemplated the lack of nuance characteristic of that Socialist heraldry which adorned every artifact of Regime officialdom. It seemed somehow improper for the *command authority directives* that he now held within his grasp to be conveyed in such prosaic form.

Of course, at Maltsev's level of command authority, evinced not merely by a Marshal's rank but also by the presence of the other men within the "conference hall" of the bunker, such formalities would have been superfluous. He found himself among none other than Yuri Andropov, General Secretary of the Communist Party of the Soviet Union; Dmitry Ustinov, Minister of Defense of the USSR; Erich Honnecker, General Secretary of the Socialist Unity Party of the German Democratic Republic; Wojciech Jaruzelski, First Secretary of the Polish United Workers' Party; and Otto Remer—a man with neither title, portfolio, nor since 1945, national citizenship or discernible allegiance, yet who was most responsible of all the men present for the decision to initiate the plan known to them (and select individuals designated as Wartime Command Authorities) as *Case Blue-Ryan*.

As the gravity of their purpose began to penetrate his consciousness, Maltsev pondered the irony of the informality that reigned among these tyrant-functionaries—deference to, even acknowledgment of, martial rank and seniority of office were not observed. Within this exclusive and godlike fraternity wherein membership conferred dominion over strategic nuclear warfare, it was understood that strict adherence to chain of command conventions would be gauche, even vulgar; thus, a tangible equality prevailed among these architects of *Mega-Death*—not unlike that described by pagan scribes and poets as prevailed between Olympian deities or, perhaps more appropriate, the parity of status between the Luciferian cavalrymen of Scripture; ruthless beings prophesied to arrive in advance of God's adversary, emergent before the vermillion fire of Hades, presaging apocalypse in the wake of shattered seals.

Maltsev was pleased that his hands did not tremble as he read aloud the protocol script that called upon the decision maker to initiate Case Blue-Ryan. He had devoted a three-day vacation (a princely luxury, in his estimation) to recreation and bonding with his bride and their young children, cloistered at Maltsev's *dacha*—a sprawling yet not garish mansion in Sochi that had afforded him much needed peace of mind on these occasions. There was no reprieve, however, for Maltsev during this final retreat.

Remer had called upon him at the *dacha*, his presence exuding a sinister though invisible aura—Maltsev never failed to notice the fear and abject submission in his wife's body language any time Remer was present. In the way intrinsic to women, Aisha Maltseva was a metaphysical weathervane, intuiting ruthlessness and malevolence in others. Remer wore his capacity for controlled violence on his sleeve—intuition, feminine or otherwise, was not needed to perceive it; the detachment and precision with which he both "wore" and employed it made an impression on those sensitive to such nuances.

On that day, Remer had walked with Maltsev in the garden, and had gifted him a leatherbound book, inscribed by its author: a theorist of *Jihad*, of political philosophy, of the histories of the races of men, all and sundry. Remer knew by his own legendary intuition that his comrade was an occulted Muslim. He knew what sort of appeal would fortify Maltsev to execute an order diabolical in consequence if not in deed, an order that would realize what up till then had been only speculation on the outcomes of game simulations—outcomes numeric and sanitized by euphemism.

Remer had divined Maltsev's frailties—only an appeal to serve God unconditionally, issued forth by a killer of unimpeachable faith, could let Maltsev rationalize that within days his executive decision would culminate in hundreds of millions of the *Mega-Dead*. God's will was Armageddon: to prostrate oneself before it was piety; anything else was cowardice and complicity in one's own damnation.

On that day, Tamerlan Maltsev, Marshal of the Soviet Union, with an icy countenance born of certainty that he was acting as the sword and arm of his Creator, issued the order for a pre-emptive *decapitation* strike against what was then the United States of America, followed 41 minutes after by a secondary fusillade of intercontinental range missiles that struck every countervalue objective on the list generated by the Strategic Rocket Forces' targeting computer.

It was Christmas Eve by the Gregorian Calendar—a moment that stopped time. A moment wherein millions of human thoughts, motives, and ambitions ceased instantaneously. It was the day the world was born, its birth cry a hundred silent flashes, hotter than a hundred suns.

ZONE ASSAULT

In the desert I saw a creature, naked, bestial,
* Who, squatting upon the ground,*
* Held his heart in his hands,*
* And ate of it.*
* I said, "Is it good, friend?"*
* "It is bitter—bitter," he answered;*

* "But I like it*
* Because it is bitter,*
* And because it is my heart."*

Stephen Crane, In the Desert

O N E

LOCATION: Sorelia, Alpha Akron
YEAR: 2999 AD (1016 AWD)
DATE: April 19-20

IN THE BEGINNING, THERE WAS ONLY VICTOR. Neither genius nor imbecile, intellectual nor proletarian. Not a lover who had inspired longing in the hearts of sensitive yet brutal men and sighing girls in the prime of their fleeting wildrose beauty, nor a killer who tallied the destruction of human lives by his dainty hands with the savant enthusiasm of the statistician or birdwatching hobbyist. Victor Francis von Leers was none of these things because he was all of them. And the less human Victor became, the more completely he came to instantiate these terrifyingly human characteristics.

Victor, like every Executioner (soldiery had been formally done away with over a century before his birth), was wont to infer the wishes of his masters—directives masked in euphemism and purposefully occulted by subcultural dialect. People who loathe the Executioner in all times, in all venues, among all races and tribes, assign him a moral imbecility, a servile and cultivated ignorance, or an atrophied or undeveloped humanity, in order to explain his dog-whistle perception of the blood-pearls concealed by the shell of superior orders.

In reality, his aptitude stemmed from nothing objectively identifiable; the Executioner's aloofness was coupled with an overly pious aversion to acknowledgment—let alone discussion—of his vocation by any means save for oblique reference, innuendo, or conspicuous omission. Acts in the service of God—just as the name of God Himself—were never to be described in the debased, feral dialects of men. Victor knew, with that unreasoned assuredness that only zealots can muster, that of all His children, God especially loves the mujahideen who sacralize the soil of the myriad worlds of His dominion by the spilling of blood—and of these pious murderers, the Executioners were His very favorite sorcerers.

All of history up to the moment of his conception had conspired to create Victor. It caused his father to be garrisoned to an Off-World killing field—a forlorn outpost where the man was gifted a terrified, virginal woman-child by her even more terrified mother and father, refugees fleeing a tsunami of murder perpetuated by a lumpen caste of doomed cannibals, sex fiends, and diagnosed *Terminals*. *Terminals* were a mysterious and ever-present horror on any world or station where the diaspora of man lived, died, labored, or made war in deep space. Naked, perpetually encrusted with blood and excreta, some holding severed heads aloft as trophy-totems, a smattering of self-anointed Shaman among them adorned with necklaces of ears and noses, fingers and toes, snatches and severed breasts, virtually all of them poisoned by radiation, their burned flesh emitting an odiferous bouquet of ozone, cinnamon, and decay—this epidemic emergence on the soil of Alpha Akron had guaranteed that virtually every one of the 31,403 Off World settlers would perish at the hands and teeth of the *Terminals*.

At the epicenter of this pestilence, Victor's father, Victor Ungern-Sternberg von Leers, was presented with that most coveted of war spoils. The auburn-haired girl had yellow eyes, impossibly widened by both wonder and fear. Her mother began to frantically disrobe the girl to persuade Ungern to accept the gift by exhibiting the quality of her breeding stock, going as far as to invite Ungern himself, or his medical officer (the woman unaware that he had been dead for months) to inspect the girl's intact maidenhead.

Ungern read her parents' faces—any trace of emotional control had collapsed; the expressions they wore were entirely open, a primitive honesty wrought by terror. He looked upon the girl—her left hand was flush against his lapel, the fingers of her right firmly clutching the sleeve of his uniform. There was fear within the girl, but not pre-rational terror. She exuded a dignified poise of a sort that could not be affected.

The girl's mother let slip a whispered scream as a battalion of *Terminals* hurled itself suicidally across the "death strip", an aptly named perimeter that abutted the steel, lead and polycarbonate blast doors and barriers making up the frontier of the Zone Assault fortification. The damned legions hurled themselves over and over at the obstacles, all the while issuing forth a futile if vigorous war cry in unison. This was fueled not only by berserkers' rage, but by gross enlargement of the pineal gland and accompanying overabundance of adrenaline coursing through the circulatory networks of the rotted yet powerful bodies of the *Termi-*

nals. The girl herself, however, remained composed—discordantly so.

Ungern looked down into the fair girl's green-grey flecked yellow eyes—eyes neither submissively cast downward nor meeting the wordless challenge with eager surrender—and nodded seriously, breaking the compulsion to maintain eye contact with his feminine charge/war bride/hostage, and briefly but affirmatively acknowledged the mother's and father's plea for safety from the horror just beyond the blast doors of Ungern's domain.

The stoic officer, placing his arm around the gift-maiden's waist while hoisting his flechette battle rifle with the other, beckoned his three new charges—as well as a perimeter security gunner who sported a raw flash burn on the right side of his boyish face, and a brute of a senior Grade Armory Sergeant—to follow him below ground level, past the munitions depot and fallout shelters, and into the relative security of the siege barracks.

Preparing to take leave, he gently touched the girl's face as a parting gesture, awakening pangs of longing and sorrow he had not experienced in 20 years. Until three quarters of an hour ago, he had planned to stay on the planet's surface after verifying the departure of the last evacuation vessel bearing non-expendable human settlers as cargo, then to welcome immolation by the nuclear munitions following his order for surface bombardment by low-orbit strategic missile frigates. Now, for the first time since his commission as a Novice Executioner, he desperately wished to live. Ungern's decision, driven by passion bereft of reason, on the surface of a damned world besieged by damned savages, would touch the lives of every man and woman on every planet in the habitable universe for a thousand years to come.

ROBOTA:
THE PROUD FLESH

*And except that the Lord hath shortened those days; no
flesh shall be saved: but for the Elect's sake, whom he
hath chosen, he hath shortened the days.*

Mark 13:20

O N E

*There has emerged—particularly within the ranks of
Executioners who serve the Imperium in non-Prime
Off World theatres but also among a coterie of Quantum Immortals who seem to covet personal political
power—an unorthodox perspective on historical ques-
tions. This perspective is grounded in an arcane style
of religious thought. It posits that the Third World War
and the megacide of over one billion human beings was
ordained by mystical causes or fates. Presumably, these
have been wrought by a supreme being who saw fit to
cleanse man's dominions of regressive, dysgenic, and
de-evolutionary features and tendencies by way of a
massive, punctuated, destructive event.*

*Consequently, we see a sort of inverted martyrdom as-
signed to obscure figures within the political and military command and control structures of the combatant
states. This martyrdom is premised upon the idea that
these figures were, in fact, guided by an extreme type of
religiously driven, mission-oriented purpose—and that
in order to fulfill this mission, they successfully pene-
trated the technological and bureaucratic offices of the*

ancient states in which they lived solely to thwart the stated goals of the ruling regimes. This culminating in a conspiratorial program of the annihilation of the existing global political structure in unrestrained planetary nuclear warfare that they themselves had carefully and deliberately instigated.

Internal Memorandum, Bureau of Public Information, Terran Imperium. Autumn, 3005 AD

LOCATION: F.O.A. POSEIDON, IN ORBIT OF
  TRITON
YEAR: 3033 AD (1050 AWD)
DATE: NOVEMBER 9

ON THE 9TH OF NOVEMBER, 3033, ZARTAX WAS born under conditions of creative destruction. Victor Von Leers died to facilitate his birth on that date. Surgeon Minister Woldemar al-Husseini—whose imagination and expertise had facilitated the birth of ZARTAX—died by his own hand exactly nine years later, as a delayed consequence of unleashing ZARTAX on his fellow man. LeMay Alexis Huber commented on Husseini's suicide, with characteristic aloofness, that the Minister-Surgeons are a class of men in the habit of avoiding emotional investment in human affairs to the point of callousness, yet given to a rather effeminate hysteria when forced to accept responsibility when the consequences of their actions go beyond the ordinary scope of that responsibility.

Those who knew the sad, thoughtful Arab doctor disagreed with such a punitive assessment, yet held their peace scrupulously. Taking exception to an opinion issued forth by Huber was not against the law, and technically it was not even insubordinate. It was, however, understood that indulging in this sort of sentimentality, that courting such controversy, was unacceptable. It called to mind the grotesque, infantile customs that had eliminated philosophy and learned discourse from public and intellectual life, those symptoms of the decadence, rot, and concomitant tendency towards racial suicide that had extinguished high culture and meaningful human endeavor in the decades prior to WARDAY.

What is indisputable is that the grand ambition of Woldemar Mohamet al-Husseini was animated and given form by three millennia of collective human ambition. Thousands of years of man's grandest designs and gravest mortal sins conspired to create ZARTAX. The cumulative weight of this historical sequence concluded in the events then developing as Woldemar al-Husseini, surgeon-officer of the *Ministry of Surgery and Medicine, Directorate of Biomechanical Engineering, Epigenetics, and Applied Surgery*, observed the broken body upon the levitating surgery platform before him.

The Surgeon was aghast at the state of the subject. Not, of course, because he was susceptible to the ordinary shock that befalls the uninitiated on seeing human bodies torn apart—whether the pathetic remnants be savaged by constellations of haphazard wounds wrought by shrapnel or proximity to nuclear attack loci, or ripped into unrecognizable shavings of pulpy biomass by small arms flechette munitions of the sort utilized by *Executioner* platoons.

Ministry-ordained surgeons underwent psychic conditioning and therapeutic-eugenic selection to purge them of those emotional and intellectual frailties that might give rise to empathy, disgust, or horror, and so compromise their ability to realize mission objectives. Such was the strength of this regimen that it could not even be overcome in those cases where the face of a beautiful youth had been destroyed entirely by a frenzy of hacking, slashing, and chewing at the hands, blades, and incisors of *Terminals* (as those in the final phase of *space sickness* were colloquially known by both men of caste as well as commoners). Rather, Husseini was stupefied by the fact that the body before him was still alive and respirating unassisted.

The Arab surgeon—being intellectually curious as he was, coupled with his *information clearance* level along with the statutorily dictated competence demands of his profession—was well aware that genetically engineered humans with the ability to recover from mortal injury were not uncommon subjects for a Minister Surgeon to find himself standing over in a bomb-proofed underground surgery, or a makeshift field hospital-morgue hastily constructed in some Off-World prefect slated for *Zone Assault*, or a quarantine due to military emergency or epidemic *space sickness*. This, however, was something entirely different. Husseini instinctively discerned it.

The broken martyr laid out on the cold table, his breathing as deep and steady as a well-nourished infant's or that of a long-term coma victim, was delivered to Husseini's examination table by a precise movement of the cold hand of destiny—a mechanical movement of physical matter that was but one constituent of an inscrutable constellation of causal variables and discrete effects; cumulative processes implementing an eternal historical process—a process that the augur-mystics, cloistered in their Venusian sky-city arcologies, would identify as the willful hand of the Creator revealed in the conspiratorial designs and affairs of men. Woldemar Mohamet al-Husseini, for the first time since he was a small child, solemnly uttered a desperate prayer—swearing atonement before a just, yet jealous Creator, and begging forgiveness and deliverance in virtually the same breath.

T W O

VICTOR WAS LOST IN WHAT MUST HAVE BEEN A fever dream—crashing through frozen obstacles before tumbling down on to the unforgiving permafrost. He was restrained by neither bond nor paralysis, yet his back felt as if it were about to break. Every joint, each discrete point of insertion in his powerful corpus was inflamed with pain—desperate, searing, morbid pain. In the blind-yet-sighted dreamscape of his mind, he was thrashing madly forward, colliding with walls of glassine ice. Bile emerging from his esophageal opening spilled forth an evil taste, exacerbating the reflex to wretch over and over again. The inability to swallow, despite the torturous presence of a bolus of mucosa in his upper throat, added to the vile symphony of intolerable sensations.

There was no reprieve—not even momentarily. Every window-obelisk of crystalline frost that Victor smashed only caused his nerve endings to deliver a merciless binary shock-spasm to further batter his system. Cursing, irrationally, his eugenically cultivated genome, his surgically and biochemically augmented physicality for precluding the possibility of passing out due to shock, exhaustion or non-mortal injury, he longed desperately for reprieve. His body cried out, craving the synthetic beta-endorphins that he and every other *Zone Deployed* Executioner was addicted to from their first day as a Temple Novice.

Accompanying the physical agonies of endorphin withdrawal was the *fear*—a primitive, mortal terror. A fear unendurable, augmented exponentially over dozens of nearly doomed missions. A fear buttressed by millions of seconds of punctuated horrors witnessed, psychically lethal from the screams of a hundred, a thousand, ten thousand victims. Men and women flayed while conscious, scalped as their eyes, widened by coursing adrenaline, rolled back as if with the blade as it ripped into the hide covering their skulls. Boys and girls—barely into pubescence—with their softest, most delicate orifices brutally torn to shreds by the engorged proboscii of *Terminals* relentlessly thrusting into their bodies with a rage that only the mindless idiot-berserker can muster.

A fleeting glimpse of purposefully suppressed memory—of aiming his battle rifle at the temple of a girl-child, barely past infancy, her cherubic hands pinned behind her back, bound at the wrists by concertina wire. Victor, the young virgin-executioner, bears witness as the doomed child is bent over a makeshift barricade of human-corpse sandbags, brutally manipulated at the base of her ivory-white neck by an impossibly muscular *Terminal*. For the final time in his human life, Victor endures rage and sorrow as his dilated pupils mirror and frame the radiation-sick, blood-drunk man-beast positioning himself to violate the child from the rear while slashing her throat to facilitate climax.

Victor Von Leers, novice Executioner on his maiden Zone Assault—knowing the victim is doomed—prepares to spare the girl. With the gift of death delivered by a flechette that will penetrate her brain, she will die as purely as she lived. The flash of a tactical nuclear round. The scent of ozone. The sensation of heat upon his face, despite being fully armoured in battle dress. The newly blooded killer-priest, the young God of death has not yet learned the icy detachment of his Apache and Aryan forebears, the aloof poise of the master-slayer that makes the *Executioner* a *killer angel* among ordinary mortals.

The armored and now blooded youth feels the firm but conciliatory hand of a brother Executioner upon his shoulder as he regains his senses. His thumbs are wetted in gore, having been plunged into the eye sockets of the simian *Ter-*

minal, the man-monster's fate sealed when he continued to pursue coital assault on the infant girl to whom an equally murderous, yet saintly, man-child delivered the gift of honorable death.

Deprived of the augmented capacity to suppress an infinity-reel of atrocity projected before the mind's eye, Victor's inner constitution collapsed before the awesome, megalithic power of the Beast with a thousand faces. He threw back his powerful neck and silently screamed. Only at that moment did the fallen *Executioner* come to realize that he was not asleep, nor was he awake and hunkered below ground level, enduring the blackness of Zone Assault upon a sunless battlescape—nor was he enduring the temporary blindness of exposure within a biotoxic battle theatre.

The thrashing, desperate, and primitive trauma of endorphin withdrawal shocked him into the realization of a new horror—Victor's body was entirely broken, and what he had taken for the nitrogen ice layering the frozen ground of Triton was, in fact, the cold steel of a mortuary slab.

SEED OF CAIN:
THE IMMORTAL HYDRA

The number of different aspects that the face of a man has assumed may be taken almost as a physiognomical measure of his [...] genius.

Otto Weinenger

Serial killers do on a small scale what governments do on a large one. They [serial killers] are a product of our times and these are bloodthirsty times [...] You don't understand me, you're not expected to, you're not capable of it [...] In the end, we all die and nothing really matters.

Richard Ramirez, the 'Night Stalker'

O N E

The phenomena that constitute what has come to be known—in scientific quarters as well as colloquially among all castes and classes—as 'Quantum Immortality' are, in actuality, no such thing. The application of floating signifiers, often obliquely related to esoteric topics of theoretical science, is a tendency born of conceptual biases—biases that emerged in the middle decades of the 21st century as the apocalyptic terrors of the Third World War remained in living memory, albeit as an aged pastiche of cataclysms, metaphors, and revelations.

The idea among learned men, in both government and

scientific corridors, was to replace religious belief with a complete system of rational objectivity, and to abolish the consuming and furious impulses that move men of faith to Jihad and myriad other modalities of pious cruelty. Nevertheless, it was understood, then as now, that men and women, be they plebeian and vulgar or superior and exceptional, require edifying mythologies to give formative aesthetic qualities to ethical systems.

Thus, early understanding of the potential of epigenetics and the heritability of the discrete, individuated personal consciousness—and most significantly, the continued survival of this consciousness upon the death of the physical body—was imbued with an obfuscatory mysticism.

Doctor-Professor Woldemar Mohamet al-Husseini, PhD, MD, Quantum Immortality, Eugenics, and Military Technology, 3017 AD

LOCATION: CHICAGO, ILLINOIS, UNITED STATES
YEAR: 1982 AD
DATE: SEPTEMBER 15 (WARDAY - 464 DAYS)

BUI FANG "BILLY" WONG CONTEMPLATED THE DRIED blood underneath his otherwise meticulously manicured fingernails. Billy was attentive to minutiae in ways that rendered him abnormal in relation to his fellow man. In fact, his every trait—be it as prosaic as a personal hygiene, an aesthetic preference, an eating habit, a manner of speech, or something as remarkable as the capacity to choke the life out of a perfect stranger (man, woman, or child, although Billy preferred women) without a pang of remorse—was a testament to his abnormality.

Perhaps even more rarefied than his compulsive bloodlust was his mind. From just under two years of age when he attained literacy, he could consume, analyze, interpret, and recall with perfect fidelity massive volumes of data with such precision that those few who bore witness to Billy's intellectual habits were prone to misidentify him as either a savant or, if they were intellectually primitive, some type of shaman-magician. Billy Wong was neither of these things.

Billy Wong was the son of a doomed Nung Chinese mercenary whose destiny was to be unceremoniously slaughtered by teenage executioners in the blind service of the Khmer Rouge. His mother was a Montagnard woman-child. Much later in life, as she entered middle age in a land as barbaric in its own way as the land of her birth, she came to believe that Lucifer had been granted ingress to her body and to this world when she had been impregnated by Billy's father. Probably, she reasoned, as punishment for the grave sins committed against God and man by the latter— sins that cried to heaven for vengeance, sins so depraved that even Billy's father meeting the Creator upon being blinded, castrated, and skinned alive by the *Red Khmer* could not be sufficient atonement.

Billy, like his long-suffering mother, was a refugee—afforded passage to a country that had nurtured and refined his father's killer instinct in the Godless manner that all successful Governments condition men in furtherance of their own perennial sins. Billy was an autodidact who had mastered the English language within three months of his arrival upon American soil at age fourteen, and in so doing had eradicated any semblance of an accent. Billy was a dropout who had left school at age sixteen despite a perfect score on both of his college entrance exams. Billy was an addict—he required heroin to live, if not physiologically than metaphysically; to find himself in withdrawal was to find himself cast into a tangible as well as conceptual Hell.

His existence was ordered by, bound to, and defined by this unsatisfied need. Billy was a slayer of women. His need to possess a woman, to penetrate her, to experience her physicality and psychic traits *in extremis*, and ultimately to take her life and thereby own her, body and soul, for eternity—this was the only passion within Billy's inner blackness that competed successfully with the voracious demands of his narcotic addiction.

Billy scraped the dried remnants of reddish and ochre from his fingernail with a poorly constructed folding buck knife that he had stolen from a convenience store in Chinatown. A glossy Confederate flag decal was affixed, off-center to the handle. Billy's attention was singularly drawn to the saltire at the center of the standard. He had always been transfixed by geometric shapes and representations, his mind incessantly tracing the symmetry, or lack thereof, of objects and organisms and the spatial relationships between them. It was as if he were taking notice of the limits of physical reality at all times, unconsciously positing himself outside of it—imagining himself as without extended physical presence, as representing an ethereal demonic essence, a death-god with the power to manipulate matter around him, with the power to pass through concrete or steel to penetrate, to crush, to pulverize, to slash, to sever bone, tendon, flesh, ligament or cartilage.

It was moments such as those, when he felt he was emerging before a metaphysical vista, that he most sharply felt the cold and monolithic brutality of withdrawal sickness. It dragged him from the radiant warmth of sanguinary mania and hurled him into a domain of suffering so absolute and unremitting as to overwhelm the human imagination.

It defied reason to think, as Minister-Surgeons often pedantically declared, that such pain could be generated merely by the nervous system's bioelectrical impulses. Billy felt the early pangs of the ever-familiar agony—sweat beads slowly slithering between his shoulder blades, leaving a trail of what felt like slimy frost in their wake. A strange, tingling ache around his Adam's apple jolted him slightly. He caught a glimpse of his haggard and Stygian pallor in the tarnished mirror abutting the sink over which he wearily hunched. He swallowed hard.

The washroom of the Pal-Waukee Matinee Theatre was perpetually filthy and evil-smelling, but it offered Billy a warm, comforting familiarity, and practical safety. The theatre manager on duty had never once disturbed Billy when he was shooting up in the one toilet stall with a functioning lock, either to pre-emptively stave off, or to deliver himself from, the terrible sickness. The theatre also served another purpose. Billy would not infrequently pilfer merchandise from store shelves or make off with car stereo decks to fund his insatiable habit, and on those occasions when he had reason to think that one of the myriad police patrols might be seeking to take him into custody, the theatre made for a convenient, reliable refuge.

Regardless, Billy was in the habit of spending the hours from late morning, after procuring his daily fix, until the afternoons and early evenings taking in double-features at the Pal-Waukee.

The theatre was a *grindhouse* that specialized in slasher and *Mondo* features while exhibiting an occasional foreign feature to maintain the fiction of the establishment as a venue for arthouse selections. With cultural preferences dictating the taboo on actual pornography (outside of the cloistered urban Rush Street shops whose stock-in-trade was exclusively such material), the Pal-Waukee's proprietor settled on *slasher* and vigilante-themed pictures as the featured weekday reels.

Of the currently featured movies, Billy's favorite was *Halloween II*. In recent days, Billy had viewed the double bill of *Halloween II* and *The Exterminator* no fewer than four times, finding the former particularly stimulating from the realism of the murder scenes coupled with the fact that the actresses were frequently nude, but by the time *The Exterminator* played following the intermission reel change, he could often be found slipping into narcotic stupor. Billy did not find narratives of revenge driven violence cathartic—violence without sex was an aesthetic nullity, something that appealed to vulgar dilletantes, in his estimation. Billy considered himself an aesthete, a romantic, and a student of murder—the taking of life constituting a zenith of human experience, something that could not be extricated from its self-contained merits. Any man who had to couch his bloodlust in a redemptive moral narrative or to extricate the act from its underlying eroticism was a man unworthy of the experience.

Billy had been eagerly anticipating what that evening would bring—anticipating the *hunt* as the *Halloween II* credits rolled to the gleefully saccharine strains of The Chordettes' *Mr. Sandman.* Just as his arousal was burgeoning to the level required for the night's activities, the sickness arrived furiously, with a cruel urgency that was unusual. A genuine panic took hold as sharp and unforgiving cramping laid siege to Billy's guts.

On those occasions where he was too addled by the sickness to steal or otherwise prowl the streets in search of relief, he would cloister himself in a corner abutting the kitchenette of his mother's tiny apartment in Little Saigon. On such days his mother, out of abject fear of—and loyalty to—her son, would lay out a bedroll and tend to him as he writhed and cried out in agony.

As Billy gripped his lower belly he faded in and out of momentary fever-dreams—psychic vision quests through terrifyingly bleak, blue-white tundra, oceans of frozen nitrogen beneath alien skies dominated by Neptune's rise. These landscapes were stalked by creatures more savage than himself, machine-men whose exotic, hybridized anatomy—for reasons not rationally explicable—afflicted Billy with a fear that caused him to whimper aloud and tremble.

His mother was a primitive yet sublimely insightful woman, capable of perceiving phenomena that "civilized" peoples no longer could. She knew that the belly was the seat of the spirit-element within man and that dreams were the domain of the world beyond, visible only to the *third eye*. And in these moments, his mother would burn incense and pray over her Luciferian son, appealing to Christ, the Father, and the Blessed Virgin—as well as the ancestral spirits invoked by the Shaman among her mountain-dwelling forebears—so as to ward off the evil that possessed him and stalked her home when he was present like a Stygian fog upon the blackened water. Unbeknownst to her, mankind severally would face judgment within months, although the historical purpose of the evil manifest in her progeny and bloodline would not be revealed for another thousand years.

ZONE ASSAULT

History is always written by the victor and histories of the vanquished belong to a shrinking circle of those who were there.

> *SS Standartenfuhrer Joachim Peiper*

I salute the light within your eyes where the whole universe dwells. For when you are at that center within you and I am at that place within me, we shall be one.

> *Crazy Horse*

You can abandon your own body, but never let go of your honor.

> *Miyamoto Mushashi, The Way to Be Followed Alone*

T W O

LOCATION: S.S.A. Irminsul
YEAR: 3006 AD (1023 AWD)
DATE: October 30

Ungern seldom contemplated his decision to take a bride and become a father. This, of course, was a repudiation of his vows, and ended his tenure as a *Murlyr Caste* Executioner, commissioned by direct Mandate of Imperium both to carry out ceremonial sacrifice within imperial court and to command in battle as a Zone Assault Storm Leader. The exceptions were the now rare instances when he found himself alone—purposefully taking leave of his family and those few among the *Spaceborne* with whom he enjoyed a genuinely intimate rapport—often seated in the chapel observation deck at the conclusion of the call to prayer at dusk. Cloistered within one of the mediation cubicles, enclosed at every angle by barely discernible observatory plastic, he could hardly help but reflect upon his own discrete existence, staring outward into the sea of stars similarly enveloped by the void of infinite space.

A man with a lesser record as a full-fledged Temple Initiated Executioner would have been banished from Imperium territory on pain of death—or at least publicly court martialed and all but ordered at the conclusion of formalities to commit suicide. Ungern, however, was a special case. He had, of course, been immediately excommunicated from the Temple. He had been stripped of biological modifications performed on him following his commission as a Temple novice—although not everything could be reversed by surgical intervention, enough could be 'remedied' to render him ordinary as regards longevity, physical strength, intellectual capacity, and resistance to enfeebling conditions. Finally, and most remarkably, he had been assigned to a lifelong tenure of "service" aboard one of the Imperium Fleet's now obsolete and superfluous Fleet Space Station Arcologies.

The non-military arcologies were retained in service primarily as a benefit to the remaining Spaceborne populations who were the lineal descendants of the first human colonial diaspora. The Imperium reasoned that to force them to adapt to a planetary existence would almost certainly lead to their rapid extinction, and for this reason lineal Spaceborne were a protected ethnicity under law.

Further, the ancient arcologies were considered instructive by the ruling castes. The Mullahs considered them a direct, mortal link between God and the first beneficiaries of the Covenant. The Senators considered their existence a prime symbol of the Imperium's perennial mandate, in addition to embodying the patriotic and religious tendencies that were held, somewhat sentimentally, to exemplify the ideal human mindset.

These tendencies had ancient precedents, having developed within the minds of great Khans and *historical-cum-legendary* warrior chieftains, from golden haired, sanguinary, lustful Olympian boy-generals to the killer angel savants who presided over mechanized battlefields twenty centuries subsequent, brutally aloof yet prone to memoirs and battle manuals of ashen lyricism. First among the latter was the Teutonic warlord messiah who deigned, in emulation of Frederick II, to grant Aryan manhood an armed prophet to lead him out of spiritual (and later physical) bondage, and in so doing fanatically insisted that a cultivated, sustained peasant yeomanry was essential to an inviolable bond of *blood and soil* between the population, the territory they inhabited, and the leadership caste that presided over both. The eastern Czars held a similar idea, leading to the cultivation of a Cossack ethnicity whose role within the empire was to act as a perpetually forward-deployed vanguard of peasant-killers.

Any Executioner in the service of the Imperium could recall learning as a novice initiate what was termed *Philosophical Exegesis*, the hidden-yet-visible *"hand of God"* in history—that which had driven the apocalyptic mission of the Great Martyrs, those men who had facilitated the transition from the Devil's reign upon Earth to a just and holy order by way of cleansing nuclear fire—first among them being the one known only as *Irminsul*.

On these grounds, Ungern's exile afforded him and his family a quiet dignity that was not punitive in any day-to-day or moment-to-moment way, though it was profoundly restrictive and ultimately destructive to the will and the spirit—as by design. Ungern could be likened to a legendary chieftain of a once-proud tribe of Indian braves, now confined to a governmental reservation from which neither he nor his charge could ever meaningfully stray.

The true consequences of his apostasy would be forced upon him, to say nothing of his war bride Ayisha, in mere weeks, if not days. Ayisha was heavy with child, and the gestation period of a fetus whose mother was not only *Pineal Sensitive,* but a verified carrier of epigenetically significant traits was profoundly abrogated. In the case of Ayisha, Dr. Al-Husseini firmly believed that her genetic anomalies included the potential for full heritable transmission of discrete consciousness beyond physical death—*Quantum Immortality* as it was named colloquially, and increasingly among learned castes ordinarily averse to adopting such jargon. In other words, the child could very well be a rare, successfully engineered being with the capacity not only to fully access, experience, and embody an inherited consciousness but to transmit it to lineal descendants.

These rare circumstances, coupled with the fact that Ungern himself was the product of a similar genetic engineering program—one specifically tailored to generate specimens for Imperial service as Executioners or cloistered Augurs—made inevitable a cruel reality. When the child arrived, the newborn boy (the sex known by Ayisha within weeks of conception without need of ultrasound nor diagnostic hologram) would be ripped from his mother and father and delivered into lifetime bondage to the Imperium. During his increasingly frequent psychic sojourns spent staring from the observation chamber into the infinite maw of the cosmic abyss, Ungern had come to realize a subsequent irony. He, Ayisha, the entire tribe of the Irminsul Spaceborne, all the subjects, slaves, and nobles of the Imperium, the Caliph himself, and every living thing in the habitable universe within the anthropic horizon—all were fated to be delivered into the bondage of a superhuman Madhi tyrant, a tyrant who would begin life upon emerging from his wife's womb within days, if not hours.

Ungern suddenly felt profoundly aged and profoundly frightened—a fear that made him sick at heart. A fear that robbed a man ordinarily without frailty of his strength, his dignity, and his faith in the hidden-yet-visible hand of God. As a barely perceptible, involuntary whimper escaped the old man's lips, he uttered a prayer offering absolute contrition and begging forgiveness for himself and his bride.

ROBOTA:
SHEDDING SKIN

What's so noble about being dead?

> *Dalton Trumbo, Johnny Got His Gun*

It should be understood that doctors did not want to damage their patients—as a profession, they were sworn to do no harm—but if they committed dastardly acts, they were more easily pardoned if something positive had come of the exercise.

> *Allan M. Hornblum, Against Their Will: The Secret History of Medical Experimentation on Children in Cold War America*

T H R E E

LOCATION: Paradise City, Atlantic Prefect,
 Planet Earth
YEAR: 3034 AD (1051 AWD)
DATE: April 20

Husseini contemplated a clichéd yet timely observation that he had come across in a Shakespearean drama from his student days. The dialog had suggested, with characteristic lyricism, that every man of noble blood who fathers a male child at some point comes to gravely fear his heir. To the diligent student of political affairs, it cannot, after all, be anomalous that Alexander—the greatest king and most inspired general who ever lived, and who was tutored by the greatest ethical teacher who ever lived prior to the birth of Christ—ascended to an already gilded throne by an act of patricide.

Of course, what distinguished the trials and anxieties of ancient noblemen, as well as those of the dramatists who memorialized them, was that however great, these men were merely mortal—as were their offspring. The fear that swelled like a malignant bolus of tumor in the breasts of kings upon observing their ferocious progeny now grown was at least tempered by one thing: the fact that their Oedipal rivals were mere men and in no way Godly nor more than human.

As he sat in the lotus position, Husseini shuddered at the realization: these ancient kings and their progeny were not genetically engineered and cybernetically altered to survive for centuries. Their skin was soft, easily injured, and deteriorated rapidly after childhood—their resplendent, fearsome, almost robotic appearance when fully armored for ceremony or battle was merely an illusion, albeit one brilliantly engineered. Beneath their ornate gladiatorial ornamentation was ordinary human flesh and blood. Flesh not crafted from iron or steel—nor from kevlar or platinum. Their bones were brittle and became arthritic in middle age—their skeletons not made of titanium alloy nor fortified by exotic, man-made polymers. Homicidally jealous of their father's power and wealth, ferociously covetous of his harems, envious of the legions he commanded as these ambitious princes might be, nonetheless they were merely jealous men. They were not thinking machines or self-aware weapons of mass destruction, nor robotic gods of death with potential active service lives measured in centuries. They were not genetically engineered for biological immortality. They had nothing in common, save perhaps for vocation, with the Executioners of the cybernetic age that was now reaching its zenith in the first centuries *After* WARDAY. They were, in every way, just as weak of mind and constitution as the fragile men who had sired them out of desperate instinct to do something—anything—to mitigate the cruel brevity of their own lives, motivated by the perennial conceit that one can defeat death through procreation.

Husseini had, in spite of himself, acquired the habit of addressing the awe-inspiring organism now before him—a diabolical being that fate had ordained him to *sire* in some metaphysical way—as "ZARTAX". The project that had created it had supplied the acronym. Husseini had noticed it prominently lettered on the cover page of a sealed, *eyes only* document, before even reading the contents: "Zone Assault Robot: Type eXperimental"—Project ZAR-TX.

There was something brutal in the bureaucratic argot used by the official fiefdoms of the Imperium. Particularly by the Security Echelon Corps of Executioners, from the runic lettering indicating SECE service and concomitant *Initiate* status, to the stylized *totenkopf* badge that adorned the lapel of an Executioner's priestly uniform in lieu of a more conventional indicator of rank. Despite the abolition of armies and the soldiering profession, the Security Echelon continued to earnestly mimic the aesthetic trappings of ancient armed forces—at least, of a few elite formations known for both lethality and religious commitment, for ceremony and fanaticism.

Husseini vividly recalled an experience he had as a boy of eleven years of age. He had already been slated for a career as a Minister-Surgeon; his father was a Surgeon of some repute and the young Husseini had been subjected to the *Professions Aptitude Psychometric Analyses*. All boys were tested at eight years of age, girls at seven, the only exception being those who carried the trait of *Pineal Sensitivity* and thus the ability to access ancestral memories. Such youths were sent Off-World, studied incessantly, and on reaching maturity, mated with those who carried the same traits. The purpose of these efforts was to identify and ultimately cultivate the capacity for an individual human consciousness to be transmitted through biological heritability.

The young Husseini, being neither *Pineal Sensitive* nor carrying any traits coveted by the Imperium in its quest to realize *Quantum Immortality*, was subjected to the primary educational curriculum common to all boys of superior blood. Looking upon ZARTAX, he recalled something. At the primary school to which he had been assigned, he had interfaced with a learning computer, a virtual reality cognitive sensory immersion device, the subject of study being the History of Warfare in Late Indo-Aryan Civilization. He had been marginally aware, as every schoolboy was, that a Spartan, Aryan-descended culture, in the generation before the final war and subsequent apocalypse, had sought to accomplish—albeit by the crude methods of the epoch— what the Imperium had finally achieved a thousand years subsequent.

Husseini recalled a particular image from the immersive interface—footage of the final stand of the ancient warriors of this vanquished Reich. The setting of this terrible battle was a Terran city in Varangian Europa that was then called "Budapest". These terrible warriors were, to the young Husseini, indistinguishable from the first cybernetically enhanced Executioners then being fielded by SECE. It was only on querying the computer that he realized that these apparently contemporary, gladiator-executioners of history had lived in the year 1945 AD—a full millennium before the first cyborgs, whether in the service of the Corps of Executioners or otherwise.

At that moment, Husseini the man tried to quell an involuntary shudder. The millennial death dealers of this ancient Reich that so transfixed his youthful intellect were standard bearers of a historical phenomenon that was now nearing its completion. Husseini himself was the father of a great and terrible phenomenon of pure history. The self-consciously sensitive Arab surgeon grew faint for a moment, overwhelmed as he was by the gravity of what he had ordained and the suddenness of its full realization.

Husseini battling vertigo, his chief assistant Nurse-Surgeon, a statuesque, seemingly ageless Persian beauty both elegant and savage, took quick notice, offering and then administering a combination of an ammonia capsule inhalant and an injection cartridge of vitamins and amphetamines to steady him. The world-weary Husseini regained full faculty of his senses within moments. At that instant, ZARTAX's target optics (in lieu of a right eyeball) began to glow—a green pinpoint within a deeply recessed black oval. History was once again asserting its sovereign dominion over men and their petit designs.

ROBOTA:
THE KILLER ANGEL

That is not dead which can eternal lie. And with strange aeons even death may die.

H. P. Lovecraft, *The Call of Cthulhu*

Once Chamberlain had a speech memorized from Shakespeare and gave it proudly, the old man listening but not looking, and Chamberlain remembered it still: 'What a piece of work is man...in action, how like an angel!' And the old man, grinning, had scratched his head and then said stiffly, 'Well, boy, if he's an angel, he's sure a murderin' angel.'

Michael Shaara, *The Killer Angels*

F O U R

From the inception of PROJECT: ZAR-TX, several years before the ultimate subject—even prospective candidates—for corporeal salvage, reconstitution, and augmentation had been identified, it had been determined that the chemical dependency which could be presumed[1] to afflict the subject ultimately selected for ZAR-TX would be not merely preserved but profound-

---

1 This presumption owing to the candidate pool consisting exclusively of active service Executioners with experience in leading Zone Assault operations in lieu of other Temple vocationary functions—i.e. ceremonial sacrifice, death lottery duty, judicial warrant execution, and 'FOZA' ("functions other than Zone Assault").

ly and deliberately augmented.

The formal record documenting the planning, inception, execution, and history of all matters relating to ZAR-TX was codified and maintained by the Bureau of Public Information. This record stated that, as was required by law and custom, a quorum was convened of senior jurists from the Justice Ministry, three of the most reliable Augurs then impaneled as the Quantum Immortal delegation to the Presidium Academia, along with a nominally civilian delegation of Minister-Surgeons with rare expertise in epigenetics and robotic neuroscience.

The document went on to allege that this elite coterie vigorously debated every relevant aspect of the program, giving particular attention to the ethical quagmires and technological aspects presented. This claim, however, was a carefully crafted fiction of the sort that had come to be seen, in hindsight, as habitual in the five centuries preceding—consequently disadvantaging all but the most diligent students today looking at official records consisting largely of confabulation and propaganda in lieu of rigorous historiography and accurate documentation of the processes of sovereign decision making.

The decision and order to implement the ZAR-TX program had, in fact, been ultimately rendered without meaningful debate, by the order of a single man—LeMay Alexis Huber. Huber was, at the time, the most senior Martyr Class Temple Executioner, and the longest serving Temple acolyte within the Presidium Standing Committee. Huber was also arguably the single most powerful man on the planet for the majority of the 31ˢᵗ Century AD. His power went largely unchallenged for over seventy years in large measure because of Huber's personal mastery of killing techniques; his grossly apostate, yet charismatic messianic posturing; his survival of over a dozen Death Lottery selections; and at least in part from his apparent resolution over the so-called

'Space Sickness' pandemic, profoundly destructive, and at the time as mysterious as it was menacing.

Subsequent histories, inspired by holy rather than diabolical impulses, noted the cunning of Providential reason by which LeMay Alexis Huber inadvertently facilitated the destruction of an infernal planetary government of his own devising. The pestilence of apostasy rendered him frail by his terrible and powerful creation, designed to guarantee for posterity his grip upon the affairs of men throughout the Solar System—only to witness that very creation become the instrument of God's wrath!

Zulfiqar, Aristotle Victor Harold, The Madhi Headhunter: The Prophet as Warlord – ZRTX, His Life and Times 3033–3050, 3183 AD

"CAN YOU HEAR ME, NOBLE ZEALOT?" HUSSEINI asked of the magnificent abomination, affecting the formal, deferential tone of the official dialect. "I ask again, noble zeal—"

"*Yes*," came the reply.

Its voice was clipped yet resonant, a deeply layered hiss. It caused the blood of Husseini and the four other observers to run cold. The surgeon bowed reverently, hardly noticing that the cyborg had, in one fluid motion, risen from the reclined platform and swiveled its entire torso and head rightward, focusing intently on the youngest man in the room—a robotic weapons technician named Theron.

"Allah, in his benevolent wisdom, has gifted you with new life, worthy servant of Providence. May I humbly ask, Great Assassin—"

Husseini was still speaking when he noticed that ZARTAX had leapt the fifteen feet between himself and young Theron, having run target acquisition and lethal assault protocol in a thousandth of a second. In a moment, the killer machine had broken the youth's neck and deployed a secondary weapon system incorporated into its prosthetic right arm. Utilizing a fourteen-inch bayonet with laser-augmented single cutting edge, it cut into the dead man's skull, intent on reaching the brain matter to harvest the pulverized pituitary gland for beta-endorphins, bound for the medicinal dosage chamber just below where the robot's left ear had been prior to catastrophic injury and subsequent bodily prosthesis.

Instinctively, the novice Executioner on the right flank of ZARTAX raised his battle rifle, aiming for his adversary's platinum faceplate and squeezing the trigger in a single, practiced maneuver. The robot parried with precise agility and economy of motion, in a single fluid movement severing the hapless Theron's head from his pathetic, broken corpus as flechette rounds struck his armor, ricocheting wildly about the chamber. With sickening power, the robot wielded the severed head in a crushing arc, smashing it against his attacker's face and driving exploded bone shards into the frontal cortex with such terrible force that several emerged out the nape of the target's severed neck. The Executioner remained standing despite brain death—his rifle still aloft, trigger finger depressing the mechanism until the internal magazine was emptied.

After several seconds, the man's lifeless body fell flatly backwards. Husseini vomited as ZARTAX fixed his optics upon him, still gripping a pulp fragment of the severed head. The surgeon shielded his eyes and frantically began to pray. His supplications to God were apparently answered, as the light flickered within the cyborg's optic socket and the living weapon dropped to the floor like a cast-off marionette. The observers beyond the secure cell, having activated the fail-safe mechanism, had rendered their magnificent abomination unconscious.

The Bureau of Public Information would suggest to Husseini in official debriefing that the delay of the fail-safe had been caused by the difficulty in sabotaging the cognitive and central nervous system processes of a cybernetic organism as complex as ZARTAX. Husseini, however, knew that this was a lie, particularly ignoble. The War Ministry had wanted to be certain that ZARTAX's first action upon being given life was an act of remorseless homicide.

VICTOR, FULLY CONSCIOUS FOR THE FIRST TIME since having fallen, mortally injured, while leading the *Zone Assault* on the frozen hell Triton, felt a heightened awareness within himself. A plethora of visual and tactile sensations bombarded him, punctuated by powers of observation previously unfamiliar. All this he experienced instantaneously—as a staggeringly rapid, jarring series of psychic and physical processes. At the same time, he felt frozen within his strange new body. It was as if he were altogether passive, an empty vessel—perpetually awaiting directive and incapable of spontaneous action no matter how miniscule.

As a cobra would require prey to enter its visual field to provoke a limbic response, he, too, felt capable of contemplation, decision, or action only upon perception of external stimuli—for which he felt a voracious, nearly tangible thirst. As if *information*—from the most trivial minutiae (such as the precise position of his body in space, the dimensions of the room, the color of the walls) to the most complex symbolic formula—was a necessity of living moment-to-moment, as water is to the cells of a human body, or oxygen to fuel those same cells that constitute a biological organism. It invited a peculiar, sharply intimate sense of vulnerability and embarrassment not unlike being exhibited naked before a gallery of strangers.

Concomitant was the familiar pain of acute endorphin withdrawal. Victor—having died and risen, becoming ZARTAX—had been shorn of virtually all traits excepting (and not by oversight but by explicit, purposeful design) the human frailty that had held him in merciless thrall for all his mortal life. He again rapidly scanned the chamber and remained seated.

He had discerned in milliseconds—having accessed data about the remaining demands of his vestigial biological systems—that the precious substance which so captivated his awareness could, in fact, be harvested, acquired, processed, and administered by his new body. Not only was this a potential capability of his cybernetic physiology, but the central processing unit that had been integrated into his brain structure was delicately tailored to provide an enhanced biochemical reward mechanism.

When ZARTAX identified a source of beta-endorphin, his brain matter would be drained of serotonin until the process of harvesting the coveted substance was initiated. At the moment of initiation, serotonin and dopamine would flood the brain in reward. Upon harvesting and administration of beta-endorphin from the targeted source, the cyborg killer would receive an orgiastic reward of dopamine, oxytocin, and serotonin rushed directly into his vestigial brain by the central processing unit that controlled and regulated every function of his being, organic or mechanical.

The risen Victor, now ZARTAX, immediately discerned that the substance he so desperately hungered for was contained in the soft brain matter of the other men in the room. Within his field of vision, a *heads-up display* of sorts emerged. ZARTAX's programming facilitated this comparatively primitive operation for various primary tasks: military command and control data would display immediately upon receipt to prioritize mission orders above other processes or secondary command protocols being run by the primary mind interface (*PMI*) of the central processing constellation (*CPC*). Similarly, a visual targeting assistance program would prioritize adversary targets and establish order of attack when infantry combat was within visual range during Zone Assault operations. What the newborn cyborg was experiencing, however, was something remarkably different from these other core functions.

As the *CLEP* (Consciousness, Linguistic, Executive-Functionary Processor)—a subsidiary component of the primary mind interface integrated into ZARTAX's biological brain, that regulated everything from autonomic functions to the cyborg's superhuman capacity to reason, governing his vestigial emotions and aesthetic judgments—interpreted hundreds of simultaneous data inputs from highly attuned optic and aural sensors, ZARTAX experienced a visceral compulsion to attack the humans and harvest the precious fluid-substance that would alleviate his excruciating withdrawal symptoms.

The substance that his optic sensors were scanning for—by way of electron magnification behind discrete and task-specific filters—was clearly registering (in the form of symbolic-graphic display representation) as deep within the brain matter of the humans in immediate proximity. The *PMI* instantaneously relayed the calculation that the man situated 0.67 meters from the ridge of ZARTAX's right hand was within millimeters of ideal targeting distance for secondary weapons. By the time the *PMI* conclusion appeared on the heads-up display, Theron was dead and ZARTAX was alive, having passed the first series of tests of his executive functioning protocols and command and control responsiveness with flying colors.

SEED OF CAIN:
THE IMMORTAL HYDRA

All significant concepts of the modern theory of the state are secularized theological concepts [...]

Carl Schmitt, Political Theology

What's one less person on the face of the Earth, anyways?

Theodore Robert Bundy

T W O

LOCATION: CHICAGO, ILLINOIS, USA
YEAR: 1983 AD
DATE: SEPTEMBER 5 (WARDAY - 110 DAYS)

"SAWBUCKS", CROAKED BILLY WEAKLY, HOLDING UP the tobacco-stained index and middle fingers of his right hand. Billy had copped from the kid before—rail thin, black-as-night complexion, incongruously narrow nose. The kid's boom box, perched on the stone steps behind them, was not emitting the familiar strains of *Afrika Bambaata* or *Run-DMC*—it was the President's less familiar yet still recognizable voice instead:

This is not the first time the Soviet Union has shot at and hit a civilian airliner when it over flew its territory...

"Only dubs, Chinaman", the dark youth retorted.

Billy was too weak from the sickness to roll the kid—skinny as he was, he was likely a game fighter. "Them blacks get down like a pit bull who just sniffed first blood when ya got 'em cornered", a dope-fiend Bridgeport Irishman who resembled a weathered scarecrow had declared to Billy in muted tones during his last stay in the 26th Street lockup. It was basically an accurate assessment by his own judgment.

In addition, Billy was well known at this dope spot—the corner boys called him "Chinaman" because he was the only head who copped there who could be so described. The primary deterrent to violence on that day, however, emerged from within himself. Billy's exceedingly sensitive, near-primordial intuitive capability—yet another abnormal psychic feature that set him apart from his fellow man—had been wreaking havoc upon his nervous system and what remained of his capacity for uncolored reason. It was like an emergency broadcast tone that could not be turned off —of the same sort that had become ominously familiar to every Chicagoan in preceding weeks from tests run on every broadcast network at 72-hour intervals.

The last thing he needed at this point was to pick up a bounty on his own head for bumping off some cornerboy for a few bags of heroin. Billy knew immediately that the kid was unarmed; it was inconceivable that a kid would not be strapped while posted to the corner unless he was known to be pushing product for a crew that would kill without hesitation—relying on triggermen in their ranks for whom murder was as casual and instinctive as for Billy—more so, perhaps, because for them it was an act entirely bereft of passion.

> *...we and other civilized countries believe in following procedures to prevent a crisis, not to provoke one...*

Billy shook his head, making what seemed a Herculean effort to will down the nausea overtaking him.

"Saw—"

He coughed and dry heaved, eyes tearing.

"Sawbucks, motherfucker."

Billy punctuated the phrase with a hateful glare, convinced that the double bags were lighter than two $10 hits—that may have been true, maybe not. Billy's perceptions, his rages and sorrows, his moment-to-moment affect were fueled by junk—either basking in the glow of it or writhing in the pain and torture of its absence. The kid was visibly cowed for reasons he could not rationally discern. People usually could not account for their instinctive reactions to Billy.

> *...and the heroic sacrifices of our young people serving in the armed forces who are fighting and laying down their lives in Santiago, in Nicaragua, and in South Africa; most recently in Mexico City this past November where our embassy staff and their families were brutally attacked by faceless cowards whose stock-in-trade is terror. And here, of course, the fight for freedom continues within our own borders in besieged Los Angeles...*

The kid relented, reached into his sock, and slapped two glassine bags into the palm of Billy's hand. Billy flicked a $20 bill he had fashioned into an origami frog at the kid's Adidas hi-tops. He saw the youngster furtively bend down to pick it up out of the corner of his eye as he half-jogged, half staggered back to the main drag of Cicero Avenue. His pace quickened as he attempted to suppress a severe attack of nausea. Simultaneously, a sharp spasm seized his guts, forcing him to halt in mid-stride and clench the musculature below his waist lest he involuntarily soil himself.

> *...as were our forebears. An American president*

> *who is unwilling to defend the American people and the American way of life by whatever means available, including nuclear weapons, is a President who is not fit for the office. Show me a...*

As he willed his body into manageable stasis, Billy staggered purposefully onward—his sole objective being to reach the cloistered safety of the Pulaski Street transit platform and a toilet stall to fix the desperately needed shot.

> *...these technologies are the instruments of peace, as they deter by rendering impossible the gravest ambitions of an enemy empire that is singularly responsible for virtually every act of evil committed within the political realm...*

Something transformative was taking place—forces entirely outside of himself, yet intractably tethered to what he saw as his fated role within Providential revelation, had asserted dominion over his thoughts and actions. Billy had been *aware* of this process for many months prior, yet his awareness was obscured by the winnowing effect on conscious reflection wrought by the self-absorption and petit narcissism characteristic of the insane.

What was in fact underway, although he lacked both the insight and conscience to identify it, was an awakening. Bui Fang Wong—more precisely, the version of him that had come to be upon emerging from his peasant mother's womb and that would continue until WARDAY, the vicious youth as peculiar in genius as savagery—was becoming more human. This transformative process would be interpreted centuries thence, by God-fearing men and apostates alike.

> *...and first among these defensive measures is the Peacekeeper missile system commonly spoken of as the 'MX'. The first of which has already been de-*

ployed. These defensive weapons are capable of neutralizing even the most super-hardened structures and can provide the...

Congruous with this burgeoning awareness, Billy had endured true existential terror for the first time in his life, 19 hours and 33 minutes prior. Not a simple, limbic response—the sort of fear that serves practical survival as a biologic warning mechanism—Billy was well acquainted with that fear, requiring as it did nothing more than a reptilian brain-stem structure and an intact nervous system. What he had experienced the day before was nothing like that. It was an all-consuming, mortal terror—made devastating to the youth's tortured mind and blackened spirit in part by its unfamiliarity.

...allows me to state with absolute confidence that the window of vulnerability that so profoundly threatened our country, our future, and our children's future is at an end...

Like a virginal girl-child, ignorant of both the intimacy and the brutality of human life from her tender years and purposeful sheltering, made instantly aware of such matters for the first time by violent rape—the combination of strange and terrifying emotional responses with an incongruous excitement that attends traumatic personal revelations had rendered Billy vulnerable. Had he not endured such psychic injury, he might have escaped the grip of fate on that day.

THE MONTHS LEADING UP TO WINTER OF 1983 IN Chicago were characterized by Indian summer. It was well over 75 degrees in the hours past high noon. The true season was indicated only by a low orange sun, a gallery of pumpkin faces atop porch rail balconies and poorly kept brickwork stoops, and a brilliantly colored patchwork of leaves mere days away from falling to reveal the skeletal arboretum that stands year after decade after century as a sentry corps of winter.

Billy set eyes upon her for the first time at the Pal-Waukee—it was rare to see anyone else at early weekday matinees, least of all an unaccompanied young woman. He was inspired by her almost spectral emergence, watching her through the thick, languorous haze of intoxication. The contrast between the woman-child's stygian pallor and luxuriant, impossibly red mane struck him. There was a jarring yet harmonious effect, her spectral eyes flashing hazel and yellow when the rhythmic points of artificial light from the *SPACE INVADERS* pinball machine and the always lit, always empty popcorn cart danced across her wetly glazed corneas. The whole scene contrasted sharply, supernaturally. Her dress was a bit too formal, too impractical for the grimy movie house, yet at the same time provocative—deep red turtleneck sweater, knee length skirt, high faux leather boots of the sort that women wore on the covers of fashion magazines as of late.

Billy did not believe in harbingers or spirits, yet he was not immune to the superstition of his mother's lineage. He found the girl's emergence upsetting, sharply felt but difficult to articulate. He felt magnetically, irresistibly drawn to her, yet repelled at the prospect of abiding his usual habits of predation and forcing himself rudely inside of her, then destroying her upon climax. For the first time, he felt a peculiar shame so pronounced as to be almost tangible.

Never in his life had Billy felt as exposed. In his mind's eye, he saw his skin flayed off, sheared from his body, the slightest breeze causing a cold wetness to envelop him that became intolerably painful. He reached into the front pocket of his jeans before anxiously recalling that he had consumed his last Valium tablet the night before last when the nightmares had been particularly unrelenting. He felt a sudden urge to leave the Pal-Waukee and run to his mother's deteriorating flat. The shame of the impulse prompted a brutal wave of nausea as he smelled and felt and saw his long hair, dust particles illuminated in slivers of artificial light, and all manner of microbial ephemera envelop his skinless body, coating the raw and bloody sarcomere. Just as rapidly, the dust morphed before his eyes into tiny crystalline shards—shards becoming salt, salt becoming glass. Sweat mingled with blood coated him, gluing his shirt to his heaving back, generating pure agony.

As his panic reached a crescendo of intensity, he registered something fragrant and intoxicating—lilac, cinnamon, and the unmistakable scent of a woman exuding fertility, opening as a garden does to a rainstorm, revealing its sensory delights. Billy focused his gaze; she was now mere inches away from him, her yellow-hazel dancing eyes seeking his own. He had been weeping, silently, unconsciously.

He broke away from her gaze. Looking into her eyes tore him to pieces, his chest ached sharply, violently.

"I—I saw..."

Billy intended to explain to this dark angel—this night creature that somehow, through her emergence, had allowed him to have the dreams that had been stolen from him all his life, the ones cruelly replaced with nightmares both waking and sleeping. She put her finger to his lips—it was splendidly manicured and smelled intoxicating. Billy struggled with all the might he could muster to retain what little composure dignity allowed.

"Would you like to sit with me?" she whispered, vermillion fire dancing behind her eyes once again. She turned away, somehow beckoning without gesture. He followed her into the darkness. "Beauty always destroys", a poet once said, Billy recalled. He was devastated.

Her name was Anastasia Eastridge. She was twenty-one years old and, like Billy, a harbinger of death. Anastasia drank the essence of those she destroyed, yet she was a stationary murderer. Her victims approached her, intoxicated upon discovering her in the night. She remained convinced that they destroyed themselves, as a hummingbird who drinks the nectar of a poisonous blossom—in contrast to Billy whose totem was the cobra.

Billy had discerned early on after coming to know Anastasia Eastridge that something profound was at work within himself. She had offered herself to him—like an oblation slated for sacrifice under the ceremonial knife of an ancient temple priest to assuage a sanguinary terror-god—with a resignation that was at once desperately fervent.

When he had first taken her the night they had met, the way she wrapped her limbs around him made him feel like a captured prey animal—her lips locked onto his, creating a wet seal; Billy felt as if she were depleting the oxygen from his lungs, draining his life essence. As their bodies were entwined, he daydreamed that a bluish lightning was being extracted from him (he had witnessed such a scene in a *Giallo* film about vampires from one afternoon months prior). In spite of his consuming desire, Billy feared during these moments of bodily union that this sorceress-harlot was strengthening herself as she drank of his vitality while he was rendered immutably frail by the same process.

Anastasia was the only woman Billy had ever had whom he had not paid for nor taken by force; she was the only woman Billy had ever kissed, and most remarkably, Anastasia was the only woman Billy had ever had more than once. Every other had been strangled or slashed to death at the approximate moment when Billy released his seed deep within them. Anastasia enjoyed the distinction of having survived Billy's climax dozens of times. She had taken his seed deep inside of her and been permitted to retain her life—sighing barely audibly, gracefully collapsing her own body into his, co-mingling their essences as he remained inside her long after their shared release.

Billy did not fully understand why he had continued to spare her. He had suggested to himself during his endless inner monologues that he had no choice but to let her live—*civilian* that she was. The apparent violation and subsequent murder of a North Shore college girl, and a painfully beautiful specimen at that, would not go unavenged. The police would never stop hunting him—retribution of this kind was the raison d'être of 20th century lawmen.

Destroying whores for sport or reasons of social hygiene was tolerated, if not welcomed, by the collective subconscious of the commons, and that of sovereign officialdom. In contrast, a *lumpen*, junkie Chinaman who had the audacity to slaughter a co-ed after having availed himself of her bodily delights was as born for the gallows as Anastasia was born for sensual experience.

Billy knew, however, that he was lying to himself—the reason it had been so difficult to kill Anastasia was not anything as prosaic as practical self-interest. He had become as addicted to her as to the heroin that he slammed into his veins at every opportunity. He was destined to murder her, but he could not bring himself to destroy this beautiful bitch—this baroness of the darkness whose silent dialect was pure, diabolical, and overpowering, and only discernible under cover of night—unless it was the only way to truly *have* her.

"You'll never have me, Billy..."

She would torture him as she dared him with her eyes, with her upper lip curled into a feral snarl of contempt. She would struggle under his weight, refuse to give into him— to open up to his intrusion as a defeated invader capitulates lest the adversary scorch the Earth. She had mocked him in death as she had in life—her eyes aflame, loosely focused, glazed in the ecstatic terror of death throes, pursing her smiling lips in final purposeful effort—effervescent lifeblood pouring forth out of the gash inflicted upon her soft, taut flesh.

IT WAS IN THE FINAL MONTHS PRECEDING WARDAY, during his and Anastasia's last combative couplings, that Billy's greatest desire and most desperate fear was realized. It culminated in a catharsis of orgiastic violence. It was the moment Billy had always been seeking, emergent before his rational mind could apprehend what he had done.

On the verge of climax, he had felt Anastasia's resistance begin to abate, almost imperceptibly. As she approached release, her labored breathing softened the feral expression that cloaked her delicate, feminine beauty at peak arousal. Her capacity to resist weakened; her soft lips gave way to Billy's desperately hungry tongue.

Overwhelmed with desire, feeling himself being absorbed into this virgin-harlot goddess, he slid the faux ivory handle from underneath the pillows of the bedroll upon which Anastasia writhed underneath his own sweat-slicked body. The straight razor had been reserved for just this sublime occasion. With the finesse unique to the knife artist, Billy deployed the blade with a flick of the wrist, and with an economy of motion befitting a matador, the blade slashed Anastasia's flesh down to the bone, where the narrow blade embedded in her upper vertebrae. Synchronized with the final contractions of her heart and the ecstatic, painful spasms of Billy's ejaculation, a stream of blackest lifeblood emerged from the cut in Anastasia's alabaster neck that had nearly decapitated her, and splattered across Billy's face and taut, muscular chest.

At that moment, a world—the only world in which he

had ever truly existed—exploded behind Billy's eyes, and he experienced the final visionary journey he would endure prior to WARDAY. Vestiges would remain well beyond, but it would never be as it was—the pure and uncolored intensity of the experience was not to return. In the familiar fugue, he was delivered to a hellscape of permanent midnight, kneeling upon black granular sand, beset by an impossible machine. An infernal thing, terrifying as it was ludicrously structured, as complex war implements are. It had a death mask in lieu of a face, dominated by gaping ovals that surrounded unbearably bright green

pinpoints. The non-face of the monster was framed by an enormous, tangled mane of blonde and silver hair, the incongruousness of which made Billy wretch.

In the wake of this visionary, birth-death waking dream, Billy's mind collapsed as he experienced, in equal measure, love and terror for the first time in his young life. The no-face demon thing's filthy and matted mane whipped wildly about the ganglia of wires and fiber optic tangles sprouting from a small patch of grey-blue flesh upon its neck. It raised an obscenely engineered saw blade that it had produced by rapid conjuring—its movement so fluid and swift as to be undetectable—and braced Billy's head with its free hand in clear preparation to saw through his slim neck and remove his head from his body.

Billy ached for Anastasia in that moment more than he had ever ached for anything, including the heroin. So unendurable was the pain of this loss, magnified by the novelty of the experience, that he did not even perceive that his final view of the horizon was unnaturally skewed upward—the vision of eyes set within a head no longer tethered to a body. He lost consciousness as the slaughter-machine emitted an artificially generated, mechanical shriek at a decibel level comparable to the whirring scream of a jet engine.

ROBOTA:
SHEDDING SKIN

The problem with historical memory (memories held in common by peoples over generations) is that it is essential for generating ANY meaningful prime symbols of State, of Authority, of Government, of God. It is essential to preserve the superstructure of these aggregate experiences contained within interstitial proteins of human genomes, and to draw upon this common memorial structure. This is to say nothing of the rituals necessary to facilitate veneration and observance of worship of such Totems… rituals that often require even DEEPER appeals to ancestral memory.

Yet at the same time, a people must be afforded an enduring conceptual horizon that transcends not merely individual lives but millennia! Even tens and dozens of millennia! Even the most iron-hearted, duty-bound Patriot willing to sacrifice however many billions of lives just to sustain the Executioner's ABSOLUTE and necessary mandate could never overcome the internal 'witness' present within a people of common heritage who could see beyond the black abyss of death, the impenetrable fugue of astronomical time and who, upon return from these psychic vistas wherein they'd endured terrifying initiation into knowledge of ETERNITY, would mock with a superhuman contempt any attempt at imposition of mortal terror within their hearts by a pathetically mortal tyrant!

The Journals of LeMay Alexis Huber 3023–3039
AD (1040–1056 AWD)

F I N A L

LOCATION: FOA-DZAC "Villainous Redeemer",
in Orbit of TRAPPIST 1b (39.6 Light Years
from Earth)
YEAR: 3039 AD (1056 AWD)
DATE: November 9

ZARTAX initiated CLEP protocol as he retrieved a thick ampule of synthetic beta-endorphin from a chamber in his prosthetic right forearm. He inserted it into the medication chamber on the right side of his neck, just below where his ear had been when he was a man. He felt the hot euphoria of the narcotic flood his neural ganglia—steadying himself against the wall of the armory abutting the pre-deployment repository.

It was the first dosage after a period of repose. ZARTAX only "slept" for four hours every 24-hour cycle, yet in repose mode his systems required twice that every 72 hours. Prior to Zone Assault, the repose period was extended to twelve hours. Lately, he had emerged from repose on the cusp of catastrophic withdrawal. He understood this was by design, and not merely a cruel accident of biochemistry. Having come to associate relief from withdrawal sickness with homicide, ZARTAX was becoming more and more murderous by impulse.

In the hours prior to Zone Assault, the synthetic variant of the drug that he was administered, in purposefully inadequate dosages, barely lifted the sickness any longer. Rather, it only served to render him functional enough for battle effectiveness—his efficiency increasing exponentially as he took down OPFOR enemies and hapless bystanders and tore them to pieces to access the glands deep within their brains for harvest.

That day, as on numerous other occasions when the old man was shipboard, LeMay Alexis Huber had sought out ZARTAX in the repository chamber. As the cyborg sat immobilized but fully aware, Huber had taken a knee in front of him and placed both of his hands on either side of ZARTAX's unmasked head.

Softly, barely discernibly, Huber would caress ZARTAX, as a woman might her paramour or a son that she loved deeply. It was not lost on ZARTAX as his optic circuits perceived the old man's face inches from his own that to stare into Huber's visage was to stare into a mirror—ZARTAX's ruined face, sans battle armor mask, was virtually identical to Huber's.

Sometimes in these moments when Huber's bizarre sentimentality had taken hold, he would produce vials of synthetic beta-endorphin (beyond ZARTAX's meager ration) and delicately insert them into the medicinal chamber of ZARTAX's head. The old man seemed somehow to know when the cyborg most needed relief from the agony of withdrawal. In spite of himself, and in spite of his programming, ZARTAX had come to love the old man, as much as he could still register genuine emotions in lieu of mere limbic responses of fear and directed fury.

The old man visiting, but not bearing narcotic gifts prior to this Zone Assault, presaged something. ZARTAX had not had a keen sensitivity to his fellow man when he had lived as Victor—to immerse himself in contemplation was not only unbecoming of a Martyr Caste Executioner, but it was distracting in ways that could have compromised his instincts in the heat of battle. Yet since his resurrection, he had a wealth of time to sit idly when not deployed and contemplate the humans within his orbit.

He appreciated the obvious humanity of Husseini. In the early days, the sad Arab surgeon had even gone so far as to apologize to the cyborg when repairing and refitting him after Zone Assault operations where he had been damaged. There was a female temple steward who was a Master Weapons Technician—on one occasion, she had silently crept into the repository chamber and looked upon him, then kissed his skeletal visage while a single tear cut a path down her painted face. ZARTAX felt no such warmth towards Huber, but he had come to desire the old man's company in spite of himself due to the chemical reward that was furnished by him when he would visit.

Zone Assault on Trappist 1b was not an ordinary deployment—he realized this by way of vestigial intellect coupled with this newfound insight he had gained since leaving the affairs of men behind. Huber was nowhere to be found, ZARTAX was on the cusp of full withdrawal with no synthetic relief to be had, and so an overwhelming homicidal impulse was developing. At that moment, he would have slaughtered entire legions and their wives and children in a berzerker's rage if necessary, directed by a superhuman mission-oriented focus. This was entirely purposeful, by design of his masters.

ZARTAX screamed silently for the first time since he had awakened on a mortuary slab so many years before…

SEED OF CAIN:
THE IMMORTAL HYDRA

Preserve my soul; for I am holy; O thou my God, save thy servant that trusteth in thee.

Psalms 86:2

T H R E E

LOCATION: JOLIET, ILLINOIS, USA
YEAR: 1983 AD
DATE: DECEMBER 22 (WARDAY - 48 HOURS)

THE FEAR FIRST ANNOUNCED ITSELF BY SUBTLE indicators. It did not arrive suddenly, indicated by physiological trauma. Nor did it make itself known as a loud psychic intrusion, calling Billy out of the petit death-womb of sleep. Rather, it attacked Bui Fang Wong—condemned inmate #C919034—by a thousand proverbial cuts.

As was characteristic of every event in Billy's life, his condemnation to death by judicial order was unusual and without clear precedent. Apparently impersonal forces (perceived by Billy to represent Providentially fated occurrences) had conspired to place him where he now found himself: scandal within the State Department of Corrections, a dearth of available corrections staff (owing in part to the calling up of military reserves on grounds of the ongoing global crisis), various consolidations of inmate populations as an executive response to a massive increase in criminal convictions resulting in detention.

These matters, fated or not by the Creator, coupled with an unusually high security risk designation assigned to Billy by his jailers, had landed him in a single cell, far beneath the ground level of Stateville Prison awaiting his own execution date—when he would be transported to the "death house" of Menard Penitentiary, where 24 hours later he would be executed on-site by firing squad.

There were, of course, many who objected to a miscreant such as Billy—not an ordinary murderer but rather, as the assistant State's Attorney who prosecuted his case had designated him, "a sexually maniacal ripper"—being afforded the same method of execution as a soldier so condemned by courts martial. However, those dissenting voices were largely drowned out by a competing (and far stronger) tendency in public opinion that equated moral decency with obsequious deference to declaratory judgments of State (and especially executive branch) authority.

It had been determined Federally in 1981, as the Sandinista–Cuban War[2] widened into secondary theatres in Panama, Honduras, Mexico, and Los Angeles, that capital punishment would be implemented for all political offenses involving sedition, espionage, treason, and providing aid and comfort to enemy forces by act or omission—but also for all "criminal" forms of homicide.

Further, it was declared by executive order that the only acceptable means of carrying out a death sentence—by nominally civilian court, UCMJ courts martial, or Maritime authority—was by way of firing squad. The several states of the Union, although not obligated *de jure* to implement these measures, quickly followed suit and became

---

2 The Sandinistas and Cubans being allies, not opposing combatants despite the misleading title assigned the conflict by contemporary observers.

lesser reflections of the Federal executive and penal apparatus.

Thus, it came to pass that Bui Fang Wong, criminal slayer of women, was to be executed in the means commonly afforded to soldiers, some nine years after his father, a soldier who had killed a score in counterinsurgency actions, was tortured and executed in a way most often reserved in barbaric societies for the most irredeemable criminals.

When Billy Wong arrived at Stateville, he was initially relieved—although he had emerged from the worst of withdrawal sickness, he had not yet managed to extricate himself from the still megalithic weight of vestigial symptoms. The evil legacy of the beloved poison had resulted in suicidal ideation amidst quiet solitude becoming a regular visitor—if not a permanent resident—within the young man's already frail psyche. This was a blessing that had carried him through his arrest and initial incarceration—too weak to shield himself from the boots and fists of the homicide detectives and their uniformed subordinates, unable to resist when his fellow detainees in Cook County Jail would set upon him for disturbing them with his constant retching and vomiting.

The instinct unto death and annihilation had provided him comfort when he endured remorse for what he had done to Anastasia—despite knowing during both dreams and wakefulness that his destiny, and of the one he had so loved, could only resolve in her sacrifice with her blood on his hands. And it had given him, finally, cold comfort when the presiding judge to whom State v. Bui Fang Wong had been assigned stated unequivocally, with a typical absence of finesse, lucidity, and lyricism, that the Court would accept Billy's guilty plea but under no circumstances would it refuse the State's demand for capital punishment.

So was it mandated by judgment of court that Bui Fang Wong, on November 9, 1983, was condemned to death for the murders—with specific intent, malice aforethought, and multiple aggravating circumstances demonstrative of gross depravity and contempt for human life—of six women.

The day of the sentencing, Billy's photo featured prominently on the front page of the Chicago Tribune, situated above a photograph of a Mongolian Peoples' Republic General who had, one day previously, declared unconditional solidarity with the USSR as Soviet forces clashed openly in the Kashmir with elements of the Chinese Peoples' Liberation Army. Adding insult to injury, the Mongol had declared that the battle being waged on the Sub-Continent was indistinguishable, in character and purpose, from that being waged in Panama, Honduras, and Los Angeles.

It was clear, as nuance and the subtlety of journalistic propaganda tend to be dispensed with during epidemics of "war fever", that an association was intended between the ghostly visage of Billy's face and that of the brazen Mongol field commander. But even seeing himself in the pupil of the increasingly enraged media panopticon had not stimulated the terror that he was now enduring over the fleeting moments of his remaining life.

It began with a rat. Well-fed vermin were ubiquitous in the corridors and crevices of Stateville. However, in the lower catacombs where Billy was housed—buried, as he saw it—rats were as scarce as fresh air and traces of life, but for the footfalls of the corrections officers who delivered his food tray to the door slot three times a day and perfunctorily counted him twice in addition.

When the rat emerged, it did not immediately disturb Billy's repose—it was only when it scurried towards the molded metal sink and toilet combination that abutted the steel bunk in Billy's isolation cell that he began to endure what was, at first, a sickly unease which rapidly morphed into a sharp terror.

Since Billy's arrival, many weeks ago, he had increasingly felt the oppression of the concrete and steel tomb. It seemed a weight upon his chest, limbs, and face. At first, it was only intermittently, vaguely present. As the weeks wore on, the sensation became more and more pronounced. Immediately prior to the emergence of the rat, Billy had begun suffering terrors in his sleep, from which he would wake struggling for breath and grasping at an unrelenting pressure in the center of his chest. Every muscle in his body would lock with tension as he felt as if his sternum would snap like a wishbone under the weight of thousands and thousands of tons of concrete, iron, and steel.

Sometimes he would let escape a scream in spite of attempts to suppress such pathetic vocalizations—but it mattered not. He could not choke off the sound at its source, nor could his jailers hear him.

It was witnessing the rat scurrying about in search of food morsels even when there were none to be had, and the inability to deny that he was, in fact, buried alive within the bowels of the most secure prison then in existence in the country, if not the world, that finally broke Billy's psychic fortitude, reducing him to a state of childlike terror—yet also to a concomitant openness and receptivity. In this exhausted and depleted state, buried alive and in thrall to terror, a Devil made fearful of the Hell of his own devising, Bui Fang Wong became both the instrument and standard bearer of Man's common destiny.

WARDAY: FIRESTORM

O N E

LOCATION: CHEYENNE MOUNTAIN/ALEXANDRIA VA/CHICAGO IL/JOLIET IL
YEAR: 1983 AD
DATE: DECEMBER 24

OBSERVING FROM THE VANTAGE POINT OF HIS driveway on North Van Dorn Street, Harrison Kennely descried in the pre-dawn sky a meteorite, or perhaps a comet—mistaking the exhaust of the missile for an ion tail. He was transfixed momentarily as the warhead detonated while still ascendant in a brilliant flare-out. He made a mental note to describe what he had witnessed to his lady paramour—a Treasury Department clerk typist who resided in Pentagon City—that evening when they planned to meet for dinner prior to midnight mass.

Moments later, Harrison Kennely discerned, in the blink of an eye, an indescribably powerful source of heat and explosive energy. This was the last sensation his mind would ever register, as he ceased to exist entirely, vaporized by multi-megaton detonations originating from high above— the weapons' delivery vehicles situated in fractional orbit of the Earth. The warheads annihilated the world for miles around ground zero, including where Kennely had stood. Harrison Kennely, his paramour who lived in Pentagon City, the President of the United States, his entire cabinet, and every other civilian designated as a National Command Authority had all ceased to exist at that moment.

There were no early warning mechanisms nor alarms sounded to warn the *Mega-Dead* in their last moments of life. At least, not preceding the First Strike salvo. Launched from the Eastern seaboard, course targeted for depressed trajectory, the SLBMs did not trigger NORAD early warning systems. Command and Control had failed in the one essential component of its core mission—early warning— yet the surviving forces, the super-hardened silos housing the instruments of apocalypse having held fast, performed as intended and within the hour subsequently reached their targets in retaliation.

Strategic Air Command—having become the command element of the United States of America, to the degree that such abstractions still existed—implemented an order to reconstitute forces for "counter-offensive" posture and attack, which was launched 178 minutes after the first Soviet missiles had reached their targets. At 1307 hours, December 24, 1983, Strategic Air Command general officer Howard Lister, from aboard ABNCP, issued the following statement to his battle staff and to any surviving government, military, or civilian listeners via TACMO:

> *The United States has survived the unprovoked, murderous, 'bolt-from-the-blue' assault carried out by the USSR and allies and has not surrendered. In fact, Strategic forces have performed admirably and heroically in the face of the enemy and are presently constituted to continue to wage war as needed if the enemy is, in fact, not vanquished and is committed to perpetuating aggressive war against the United States and her Allies.*

The Third World War had resolved in America's "favor"—Soviet command and control had failed under counterattack, unable to reconstitute the strategic nuclear forces necessary to issue the coup de grâce. Although its mortal enemy had also ceased to exist outside the minds of a handful of airborne war planners who, upon landing, would have all remaining delusions shattered.

ROBOTA:
SHEDDING SKIN (REDUX)

LOCATION: Trappist 1b
YEAR: 3054 AD (1071 AWD)
DATE: February 15

For the first time in what seemed a score of years (ZARTAX's internal timekeeping mechanisms having become unreliable in the absence of regular maintenance and the effect of prolonged radiation exposure), the being that was once Victor—then ZARTAX—looked upon himself in the reflected shield of a laborer's Off-World helmet.

The skull within the bulbous helmet had been bleached a dazzling *white,* and the once black spacesuit of vintage Terran Imperium manufacture had been transformed into a matted, pale grey by the giant, red Trappist sun. Even without drawing upon his data reserves, ZARTAX recognized immediately that the corpse was very, very old. The black, general service Off-World uniforms had been phased out for every vocation but Zone Assault Executioner decades before ZARTAX-Victor had entered SECE service—let alone even been *born.* It was clear that the remains had been *in situ* for at least 60 years and probably closer to a century.

There was an incongruity between this understanding and what his data reserves (albeit not updated properly for years) had revealed: Trappist 1b was not, in fact, colonized—nor even explored—until twenty-two years prior to the Zone Assault which had brought him there. Hence it was, to much fanfare, slated for colonization by the first settler population of *Spaceborne* that had left their deep space arcology to live on an Off-World planet. He was, however, shocked out of the semi-repose that facilitated rapid analytical protocol—a modality only available when *combat* functions were not being actively prioritized. His optical sensors, for the first time in close to fifteen years, perceived his own visage.

The cyborg's vestigial human brain always defaulted to a kind of primitive repose when his machine functions spontaneously engaged. The vision *shocked* him out of it. During his time on Trappist 1b, there had been multiple occasions when ZARTAX's organic mind was clearly, unmistakably, *asserting* itself in priority over the CLEP, in the compensatory manner of a man who—upon being robbed of his sight—develops a keen ear, yet altogether much more profound. The *human* within the steel, titanium, Kevlar, and plastic prison that housed the mortal remains of Victor von Leers was breaking the capability of the machine and its suppressive processes to subdue its will.

ZARTAX-Victor could sense a score, a hundred, a *thousand* permutations of thought, of emotion, of pre-rational *feeling* cascading through the CLEP firewall, like flood water crashing against a dam that has been irreparably compromised. The memory flood crashed against Victor's defensive programming structure—the Central Processing Computer issuing command after command to the CLEP, the vestigial organic brain sabotaging execution. Finally, the cybernetic features of Victor's central nervous system—interstitially woven throughout his ganglia—implemented the final *fail-safe* protocol: Victor felt his brain being rapidly drained of endorphins.

He fell to his knees, still viewing his horrific visage in the plastic visor of the ancient corpse. At that moment, he looked upon the totem necklace draped around his own neck, made of jawbones woven with rawhide human flesh. In agony he recognized the Stygian visage in the reflection—it was the face of Huber, yet also his own. Huber had created Victor—no, had *killed* Victor and then resurrected him in his *own* image, right down to his insatiable bloodlust. For the third time since death and rebirth, Victor endured abject terror—but this time he did not scream silently within the echoing chasm of his ruined mind. This time he thought only of murdering Huber and harvesting his endorphins.

THE GREAT KHAN:
THE BATTLE OF ST. LOUIS

ONE

Billy knew that something unusual was underway even before he picked up the faint sound of harried activity several feet from his cell door. It had come from somewhere beyond the short hallway leading to the tiny chamber that housed him abutting his jailers' command post. Billy had always been attuned to his environment—like a predatory fish might detect slight disturbances in the surrounding water—often before others realized anything was happening.

This had contributed to his mother's superstitious, conflicted feelings towards him from his early childhood to the present. Something was afoot, he could feel deep within his sensory ganglia—within his cells—that was both unprecedented in his short time in captivity and strikingly emergent.

What first jostled Billy out of his near stuporous concentration was the echoing report of gunfire. He discerned a single, muffled, crack of small arms discharge—followed some dozen seconds later by the more proximate and punctuated signature of shotgun fire. The guards in the central interior control tower must be firing, Billy thought to himself—they were the only corrections officers so armed.

The staccato continued for another several instants, ceasing as abruptly as it had begun. Then, stillness—a near tangible absence of sound nor movement, so complete and enveloping that Billy momentarily considered that he had imagined the gunfire and the frenzied disturbance in the stale air of his living tomb.

Billy was not certain how much time had passed when they arrived: two dark skinned, Negroid youths and a middle aged, slight, yet muscular White man. Muffled voices, punctuated in their unfamiliarity—Billy had not heard another human voice for months, save for the dull, almost imperceptible droning voice that emerged over the PA system at intervals.

"Don't let that muthafucka loose man!"

And in apparent direct response: "Ain't your call—its LaGrone's. LaGrone said to snag the kid outta here, 'long with everyone else."

"Who the fuck made him warlord? I say we bust the fuck outta this muthafucka".

"And where the fuck you gonna go? Who the fuck knows what's even left?"

"Man, I don't know shit 'bout all that—I don't give a fuck neither. Them Russians ain't shit to me, muthafucka."

"Just open the God-damned inner door—you want to take it up with LaGrone?"

Billy leaped to his feet and stood at what seemed like military drill attention. Resisting the irrational urge to straighten his state-issued shirt and denim pants, he compromised by flattening his shoulder length hair along his scalp with the heels of both palms. It was a reaction inspired neither by vanity nor decorum—rather, this occasion clearly was ordained, as far as Billy could discern.

The prescience that had loomed so very large, had been so all-consuming in the months and days before the murder of Anastasia, and had then been so conspicuously absent since his incarceration, seemed to have returned in an overwhelming, orgiastic catharsis. Billy's knees weakened, he felt a hot tension, desperate for release, between his legs, he felt his intestines contract in a single, sharp spasm. He did not breathe as he heard the key-card mechanism drive home in the electronic lock and the first of three dead bolts retract rapidly from the secure position.

The door to his cell-tomb activated with a loud mechanical whir. Billy bent his knees slightly, in crouched attack posture—although this effort was driven by the perceived need to maintain appearances. He knew that he would not be challenged by his liberators. In fact, he knew, with all the certainty of self-persuasion that his powerful intellect could muster, that who and what lay immediately beyond the doorway would worship him with the same crude, zealous reverence that all primitive men offer to their betters. Bui Fang Wong felt a single tear cut a path down his Stygian face—Providence had not only rescued him from damnation but had, in fact, anointed him as one would a favored sorcerer. It was glorious.

My name is surrounded with such hate and fear that no one can judge what is the truth and what is false, what is history and what myth.

Baron Roman von Ungern-Sternberg

It's not for me—nor any other man—to decipher why any man is chosen by the Creator to advance or create history. What exactly constitutes a 'historical' act, you ask? The foreknowledge and contemporaneous understanding—within the moment and at the point of key decision—by, and within the contemplation of, the Man in question. An understanding of both the gravity of his action and the fact that the Creator, and not the

> *Man himself, is the ultimate author of the decision to*
> *act, the 'great Man' being merely a vessel.*
>
> > *Thorpe Kilgallen, Retrospectives After* WARDAY
> > *(Date* UNKNOWN*)*

T W O

LOCATION: ST LOUIS, MISSOURI, NORTH AMERICA
(FORMERLY UNITED STATES)
YEAR: 1985 AD (2 AWD)
DATE: OCTOBER 21

"I DON'T LIKE THE IDEA OF WAITING BEYOND DUSK—
they could reinforce by then."

Billy remained silent—not acknowledging the speaker. Harris was a valuable man—the *most* valuable in some ways. Unfailingly loyal, not a coward, yet also a hard realist—Harris retained an intact impulse to self-preservation, and this tempered his zealousness in ways that guaranteed a cold sobriety in his analyses of battlefield challenges as well as political situations. Billy never gave any indication of how much he relied upon Harris' counsel, but he was certain Harris understood his privileged role within the inner circle of the de facto command staff.

Billy's affection for the man transcended appreciation for his pragmatic aptitude for battle, and for his subverting those who opposed Billy's mandate to rule. It was Harris who had granted him *life* by releasing him from the cell-tomb of Stateville—it was Harris who had saved his life in their earliest days together, as they soon discovered that survivors outside of the penitentiary walls had transformed into something horrifying. Their savage regression shocked even the most hardened killers among Billy's and Harris' *war party* out of their dazed stupor in the first weeks after WARDAY.

Finally, it was Harris, the pale Shaman, who had conveyed to Billy, in his own taciturn way, that Billy was the standard bearer of something—something ordained by a power so awesome, so remote, so unknowable that one could only prostrate himself before it and silently accept his crushing mortality and powerlessness. Harris, in these ways and others, exhibited a splendid balance of absolute fealty, unshakable faith in the mission at hand, and the battlefield commander's sense of nuance and instinct for self-preservation that categorically precluded recklessness even in the heat of passion or frenzy of bloodlust.

The nascent *War Band* he commanded made its way across the blighted landscape, holding more in common with a feature of the newly corrupted (and volatile) landscape than a willful organization of human beings pursuing a mission-oriented mandate. In quiet moments, Billy had contemplated what exactly motivated the individual men who had opposed him. Based upon his own inner monologues as well as his regular, though brief discussions with Harris on the topic of *Providence*, Billy had concluded that the majority of those who opposed him were doing so out of the most banal of habits. First among these vestigial practices was an irrational fealty to order for its own sake, and a belief that they were, in fact, carrying out the orders of an Officialdom that had ceased to exist within 45 minutes of the onset of hostilities on WARDAY.

It was as if these small minded, frightened men believed that if they were to maintain something approaching an *order of battle*, if they retained their tattered uniforms bearing the obsolescent standards and awards of an extinct modality of social organization, if they riled their troops with appeals to these abstractions, that somehow these things might re-emerge. The policeman, the constable, the middling Army captain lacked ashen lyricism in his words, lacked zeal in his actions, lacked deeper contemplation in his thoughts, so he chose to stand on ceremony by professing fealty to an abstraction that had never truly *existed* in concrete terms even in the days, months, and years prior to WARDAY, when such things appeared to be singularly powerful.

It a splendid accident of fate—a convergence of circumstances, each with no discrete causal significance, yet taken together generating a momentum towards a punctuated, ultimately immutable event. The hapless survivors of WARDAY who were making fortress within St. Louis on October 22 had either been spared by fact of residence at the onset of hostilities or had managed to make their way to the city in the weeks subsequent, owing to its sanctuary status. Their fortunes were decided months before when the end of Earthly life had not come to pass, as the zealous enemies of the Atom age had foretold if Man, in his hubris, were to opt for war in lieu of "peace". What *was*, however, emergent from cessation of hostilities on WARDAY until the present was the black rain.

When the ashen raindrops fell, it wrought a profound effect upon the survivors. Despite taking zealous survival measures during unrestrained nuclear combat, some had committed suicide out of despair when it became clear that the *rain* was likely a permanent feature of the *new* Earth. Something deeply embedded in the subconscious mind— pre-rational and symbolic—had catalyzed the despair of the unlikely survivors of WARDAY at the first sight of the black raindrops.

Those barely alive from radiation burns and sickness, the young and old, the despondent and those ecstatic with the giddiness that accompanies punctuated horror and shock—they had streamed out of their shelters, pleased beyond reason at the prospect of being washed *clean* by the rain, rinsed clean of odiferous excreta, of encrusted blood and scabs, filth and dirt. When what fell from the sky was *not* a Godly cleansing element but yet more filthy corruption—a literal *hard* rain that further saturated the body with a grime that seemed rinsed from sulfuric brimstone—it was simply too much for many of them to tolerate.

The first had been one of the guards. Billy had not known him in that reality; that now extinct version of the world that had, within minutes—seconds even, if not fractions of seconds—ceased to exist entirely. Billy had only recognized him from his Illinois Department of Corrections uniform—an older man, Sergeant. Undoubtedly close to retirement. The guard had taken to carrying a .45 automatic—not a weapon of issue, obviously a personally held armament—un-holstered.

The weapon appeared oversized in the short, gracile man's hand. He gripped it tightly, as a child might a security blanket, or an illiterate savage might a totem amulet. The guard had emerged from a poorly, hastily constructed lean-to as the first crack of thunder registered. The shattered man looked skyward, mouth agape—and what filled his maw was ashen droplets of tar. Billy was intrigued by the depth of despair that became obvious on the man's contorted face—remarkable, Billy considered, how an abject *simpleton* could be so very capable of communicating such profound, if uncomplicated, sorrow to one beholding his pathetic visage.

The twisted mask of agony gave way slowly, almost languidly, to a blank expression of thoughtless acceptance. An unmistakably *human* gesture, primitive and instinctive. Billy contemplated the peculiar irony that the most poignant of human non-verbal expression was often conveyed without benefit of an audience—he felt privileged and bemused as the Sergeant slowly, and again languidly, raised the .45 and placed it under his chin, pausing momentarily—making peace with his God in all probability, Billy mused—before annihilating the primitive visage into devastated pulp and fluid.

The aftermath of WARDAY had caused—really, facilitated—Billy's first experience of *empathy*. Not in a way that was sympathetic to his fellow man, nor that could overcome the chasm between Billy's *primary* mode of existence and the banal, largely instinctive, and symbolically populated inner lives of those around him—both those in the *war band* and the victims that those he commanded set upon on sight. In his more reflective moments, and there were many—Billy had taken to meditation to survive his tenure in his *Condemned Row* cell-tomb—he realized that his own familiarity with death, the mastery over it he had cultivated, had been ordained so that he could transition to the world of the apocalypse with what seemed like supernatural ease to his acolytes and soldiers.

ZONE ASSAULT

We do not make war, nor do we make peace—we allow those driven before us a chance to redeem their pathetic selves by bowing in reverence before the Khan. If, instead, they insist on begging for their pathetic lives, it guaran-fucking-tees they WILL suffer torture they never dreamed possible in this life, Baby. I am NOT become Death—but I am her CONSORT and her favorite Sorcerer. I shall have none other before her. Death is supreme among the denizens of Earth and the heavens—trespass against me and you offend the Grand dame whom I serve—and Hell hath NO fucking fury like the goddess reaper of souls!

> Khan Bui Fang Wong (apocryphal) at the conclusion of the Battle of St Louis, 1991 AD (8 AWD)

The finest steel has to go through the hottest fire.

> Richard M. Nixon

THREE

LOCATION: FOA-DZAC "VILLAINOUS REDEEMER", IN ORBIT OF TRAPPIST 1B (39.6 LIGHT YEARS FROM EARTH)
YEAR: 3039 AD (1056 AWD)
DATE: FEBRUARY 15

WOLDEMAR MOHAMET AL-HUSSEINI DREADED THE briefings that he was obligated, professionally and ethically, to present without exception to Senior Martyr Caste Executioner and Steward-Acolyte LeMay Alexis Huber. He never could subdue the painful dearth of moisture within his mouth, nor remedy the subtle but persistent ulcerative stomach pain that accompanied time spent in the terrible man's company—despite having performed this duty at more than three score of occasions before as many Zone Assault operations.

It seemed that every characteristic that Huber had cultivated was tailored for no other conceivable purpose than to remind one of death. All who found themselves in the presence of the aged, yet shockingly robust, physically vigorous Security Echelon Corps of Executioners commander could not help but be reminded of its ubiquity. Not merely within the domain in which Huber moved, labored and thrived—as a shark effortlessly and with evolved hyper-efficiency slices through deep waters—but to remind his hapless beholders of their basic powerlessness in the face of death itself. Huber had cultivated an arguably delusional, subconscious response, and in the minds of those within his orbit, the old man *was* death itself.

Huber's face resembled nothing if not *the* face of death. Owing to a peculiar body modification custom that had fallen out of favor in the last two and half centuries, large strip sections of flesh and tissue on Huber's face had been artfully removed to reveal the skull beneath. The alabaster exposed surface had been treated and polished with caustic agents to generate a startling optical illusion of bright, nearly vivid white bone, coated with an armoring agent that also produced a reflective sheen.

The entire left side of Huber's jawline was stripped of flesh, creating the illusion that he was perpetually "grinning", perhaps grimacing like a creature of the deep ocean—not having evolved the ability to mimic emotional responses of the sort found in higher mammals. The horror of the effect was exacerbated by Huber's left eye socket being devoid of organic tissue. The eye itself had disintegrated when, during a common Zone Assault operation carried out on Earth, Huber had opted to forego faceplate armor— as many Zone Assault leaders had done out of custom, and because there was no absolute necessity for such things owing to a breathable (if carcinogenic) atmosphere.

When the man twelve paces in front of him had been killed by a direct hit from an RPG round, the detonation shredded the man's exoskeletal armor and saturated Huber's face with a stream of boiling hot fluid that was utilized at joint insertion points of Executioner battle armor. The eye and much of Huber's once handsome face had been destroyed. In lieu of cosmetic reconstruction, Huber had simply had the flesh stripped off entirely and seemed pleased to at the pretext to revive the arcane Military-tribalist body modification practice. Implanted deep within the gaping eye socket was a bare optical sensor, visible as a dull green glowing pinpoint—Huber had also decided to forego the overlay of a cosmetic, if useless, artificially grown and harvested replacement eyeball.

Huber's misanthropy and sadism fetish—uncommon within Executioner ranks and particularly distasteful in a man who had reached Martyr caste, let alone the senior-most rank of all SECE Temple acolytes—was tempered by the fact that he exerted no effort to mask his true nature nor hide his malevolence from view. Not only this, but he was an example of that rarest of specimen, so confident in the inability of any rival to threaten him that he could quite literally wear his propensity for personal violence upon his face at all times.

DEMONIUM PEJORATIVE: ASCENDANCY

SECE [Closed] Neuralnet TRANSMISSION (*Audio Only*) of Trappist 1b Zone Assault, November 9, 1056 AWD (3039 AD):

Hodges: *"I've got a reading of elevated biotoxic hazard indicators."*

Murray: *"It's the UV flux spoofing your gear. Disregard."*

Hodges: *"Nevertheless, sir, I think ZARTAX should take point until—"*

Murray: *"*Negative*—ZAR-TX shall remain deployed for depth—and OpFor isn't going to emerge from cover if they see him forward-deployed. You take point, Hodges."*

Hodges: *"Sir, there's a reading that—"*

Murray: *"You take point, Hodges!"*

Hodges: *"Yes sir."*

Moneagle: *"We've got—movement on the ridge line. Major—major movement on the ridge line! Thermal signature of the fucking register. Sir, this is hammer and anvil ploy—OpFor at LZ plus three clicks was not primary OpFor. What kind of—this can't be a—"*

Stafford: *"Incoming! Incoming!"*

Murray: *"ZAR-TX³ execute mission orient adaptation!*

---

3 Phonetically recorded as "Zur-tix".

Deploy! Deploy!"

Hodges: "How can they—my God it's—" [Lance Corporal Hodges ComLink terminates]

Moneagle: "Abandon selective targeting! Murray! Direct nuclear fire support to the ridge! Override manually!"

Murray: "I'm hit—ZAR-TX disregard primary salvage objective! Override... Over! Override, Murray... code zee en seven seven two! ZAR-TX target everyone at will! ZAR-TX, target everyone! Eliminate—" [Armory Sargent Murray ComLink terminates]

17 Minutes Silence

UnSub (Unknown Subject): "Save. Save. Servant. Death. Izzgod. Death. Izgooood." [Artificially modulated voice transmission by UnSub. Final transmission].

I tell the squad a joke: 'Stop me if you've heard this. There was a Marine of nuts and bolts, half robot—weird but true—whose every move was cut from pain as though from stone. His stoney little hide had been crushed and broken. But he laughed and said, 'I've been crushed and broken before.' And sure enough, he had the heart of a bear. His heart functioned for weeks after it had been diagnosed by doctors. His heart weighed half a pound. His heart pumped seven thousand gallons of warm blood through one hundred thousands of miles of veins...he was a walking word of history, in the shop for a few repairs. He took it on the chin and was good.

Gustav Hasford, The Short-Timers

O N E

The failure of the Terran Imperium to subdue Trappist 1b—pursuant to ongoing, interplanetary Zone Assault directed by and on exclusive command authority of Senior-Most Martyr Caste SECE Acolyte LeMay Alexis HUBER [hereafter referred to as 'HUBER'] and the concomitant, absolute unwillingness of SECE and HUBER himself to disclose any pertinent information regarding ongoing ZA operations, mission orientation, and objectives continues to raise very serious concerns both within the Presidium in particular and the Terran Home Government in general...

EYES ONLY internal memorandum, Bureau of Public Information (Date UNKNOWN), 1057 AWD

LOCATION: TRAPPIST 1B
YEAR: 3054 AD (1071 AWD)
DATE: FEBRUARY 15

SEE THE GIRL. THE MIND'S EYE REVEALS WHAT THE mere witness cannot. She has never seen the world where her species originated—her *race* is an iteration of human biological heritage that was never seen on Earth and that has evolved an extraordinary tolerance to ultra-violet radiation. Her culture is dominated by symbols owing directly to the all-consuming, enormous presence of a gigantic red sun, the proximity of which casts everything that exists as a duplicate shadow. The Shaman among her people—among whose ranks is her own father—knows that she is fated for great deeds. Deeds even greater than the youth who are martyred—offerings to the Demonium Pejorative—the scourge of the Trappist 1b Spaceborne and the righteous sword and arm of God.

When the girl was born, her mother wept with joy. The Shaman could not hide his disappointment that his wife had not borne him a male heir, but the girl's mother had been beside herself for the duration of her long and difficult heaviness with child, terrified that she would give birth to a boy who would then be availed to the Selection Lottery.

She was and remains terrified of the Demonium Pejorative. It haunts her nightmares and waking thoughts. During the short harvest season, Janiya, the Shaman's wife, runs to their modest but immaculately maintained homestead at the first sign of dusk. She insists that she can hear the Demonium's mechanical scream as it emerges from its repose at approach of the strange evening cycle on Trappist 1b. Janiya is not ordinarily a fearful woman, but she is too terrified of the Demonium to even contemplate it. Although she shall bear no more children, and the child she *does* have is a girl on the cusp of womanhood, she cannot overcome her singular terror of the Demonium.

When it first arrived, the Trappist Spaceborne believed that it was the DEMIURGE itself, displeased by what they (the Spaceborne) had created. The Demiurge is the great architect—and like all great architects, he hates imperfection and will destroy even what he himself has lovingly created. Only the Demiurge has *seen* perfection, so only he can judge imperfection so harshly. He takes no pleasure in this, however. And that is how the girl's father, the shaman Harald, knew that the Demonium Pejorative was *not* the Demiurge—before Harald had bargained with the Demonium to spare the Spaceborne in exchange for the sacrifice of one male youth—on the cusp of his warrior's trial—each and every month by lottery.

Harald had explained to the girl out of earshot of Janiya—to even hear the Demonium Pejorative *discussed* put her into a state of terror—that he knew it was *not* the Demiurge, but rather the messenger and scourge of God Himself.

"How do you know?", the young girl asked of her father, the Shaman.

"The Demonium Pejorative *likes* to devour men because he is hungry—and the Demiurge is never, ever hungry, he merely desires perfection because imperfection is what he cannot stand. The Demiurge was here before everything, which is why he has seen everything, little one… the Demonium Pejorative has seen nothing, because he has no eyes. Do you understand, little one?"

EPILOGUE

The great Japanese poet, dramatist, postwar dissident, and (as some would argue) De Sadean madman, Yukio Mishima, described the political realm as the natural domain of the artist, and the artist as first and foremost a Partisan. Of course, to the Western observer, even if one is charitable in his critique, such a view appears profoundly eccentric. To those not so charitable, it appears positively deranged if not deliberately macabre, particularly in the context of Mishima's oeuvre. What is less controversial is the suggestion that the novel—incidentally, Walker Percy referred to the novel as the last "sovereign" art form, and thus a medium uniquely accessible to American audiences—and the novelist bring something essential to political discourse in conceptual terms. A well-structured, lovingly crafted philosophical novel can provide the reader with an experience of fantastic vistas that are both remote and unknown, yet intimately relatable and implicitly familiar. Such phantastic settings not only are cathartic—nobody need feel ashamed of their need for occasional escapism so long as it does not become an essential coping mechanism—but they provide for the exploration of values, ideas, motifs, and aesthetic renderings without resort to pedantic abstraction or absence of plausibly human ontologies.

In the English-speaking world, and especially within the American cultural context, science fiction always occupied a peculiar niche, resonant with men possessed of certain conceptual biases and ethical sympathies. Jules Verne quite clearly appealed to the original modern era "Progressives" who, owing to their self-conception as a natural and benevolent aristocracy, had a penchant for purposeful anachronism that had a deeper psychological significance than mere quirky aesthetic pleasure. Cold War America, unable to confront the reality of strategic nuclear war (and its macabre victory metrics)—a cultural reality that was parodied in an adept if overwrought manner in Kubrick's *Dr. Strangelove*—could be explored through the counterfactual scenarios presented by Robert Heinlein, whose protagonists were biomechanical infantrymen deployed by starship to hostile worlds with lakes of hydrochloric acid, carcinogenic atmospheres, and indigenous populations of 12-foot sentient insects. Heinlein's unsubtle metaphor resonated with an audience that was then quite singularly oriented, consciously as well as subliminally, towards the very real prospect of global nuclear combat wherein their lives would quite likely be cut short along with millions of others of the *Mega-Dead* who would perish in the wake of countervalue assault by Soviet or Chinese atomic weapons. As the 1950s became the 1960s and the counterculture became mainstream—to the chagrin of thoughtful people who recognized the source and implications of the deliberate subversion of the dominant culture—more "holistic" viewpoints became prominent in the better science fiction offerings. Frank Herbert's seminal classic *Dune* addressed not merely the pitfalls of technological society in Heideggerian and Spenglerian terms, but also posited a brilliant critique of social engineering. He showed how the most successful or insidious (depending on the observer's perspective) regimes attempt to direct the course of cultural development, racial survival, and eugenic improvement over not merely generations but centuries, and how such efforts simultaneously complement, collide with, and intentionally and inadvertently sabotage the best laid plans of noble houses, technocrats, and priestly orders (literal and metaphorical). He also held up the cruel fact that even the most heroic and virtuous lives of great men are condemned to resolve in tragedy, both for themselves and for their acolytes. Which brings me to an explanation of my own ambitions for this first volume of *STEELSTORM*.

As a youth I was both blessed and burdened with something of an unusually vivid imagination. By that I do not mean to suggest an inspired creativity, but rather that the fantastical vistas I imagined contained an emotional and aesthetic depth that rendered them very "real" in the way that distinguishes dreams (in waking life or slumber) from more regular thought patterns and narratives. ZARTAX originally appeared to me in such dreams—and even at 12 or 13 years of age, I recognized in some basic if as yet undeveloped way that his emergence was significant. He was the embodiment of something profound, an archetype for which I did not yet possess the conceptual vocabulary, save for that which could be rendered in purely symbolic iterations.

In a very real way, ZARTAX was both an avenging executioner (in symbolic psychological terms I realized much later in life) and a nightmare creature. He was a childhood terror of inevitable nuclear Armageddon—nourished by the strategic landscape of the era and the collective subconscious manifestation of what Toffler called "future shock"—rendered into a terrifying personage, as menacing for its exaggerated human characteristics and need for violence (both redemptive and impassioned) as for its utterly alien, mechanical configuration of both physicality and mind. In other words, ZARTAX emerged at a moment in my psychic development when I could survive his emergence, melodramatic as that may seem.

As the night of November 9, 1989, came and went, I could—as could millions of other Americans, young and old—reflect upon the form and meaning of my nuclear war nightmares. In abstract terms, ZARTAX cast a no less ominous shadow, but what he symbolized—his ability to emerge into "our" (or at least my own) world—receded abruptly. I came to contemplate potentialities—what could have been. Not merely what could have occurred in those most dangerous final days of strategic brinksmanship, but the possibility that other futures—alternative outcomes and realities—did in fact exist.

The possibility of such things is far outside the scope of my expertise, a capacity to thoroughly understand I am not ashamed to admit. I remain however a student of philosophy, as much as it is possible to pursue such things in this 21st century. This prompts me to consider that potential pasts (and futures) can be said to "exist" so long as they can be imagined, anticipated, and can determine the decisions of men (great and small alike) and thus outcomes prosaic and profound. ZARTAX and his world have been with me virtually my entire life—I could go as far as to say he has been and remains my constant companion. The vistas that he inhabits, and those wherein his absence is conspicuous, have determined the course of my life and provided a context, in myriad subtle iterations, of mortal decisions that have been forced upon me. Thus, so long as I live, so does he. So long as he features in the imaginations of those who read of him, his great and terrible acts, he shall endure. I have tried to lock him away in a proverbial ice cathedral, and when that failed to subdue him, I chose to document his many lives—as a man, as a machine, as a Messiah, as the Demonium Pejorative—and to describe, and allow those who read of him, his strange worlds. I thank you for your interest in the ongoing story of Victor Von Leers, the man who became ZAR-TX. May God bless and keep you in your journeys by ZARTAX's side.

THOMAS CYR
(THOMAS777)

AUGUST 30, 2021
CHICAGO, ILLINOIS